The
Dark

The

by
SERGIO
CHEJFEC

Dark

Translated from
the Spanish by
Heather Cleary

OPEN LETTER
LITERARY TRANSLATIONS FROM THE UNIVERSITY OF ROCHESTER

Copyright © 2000 by Sergio Chejfec
Translation copyright © 2013 by Heather Cleary
Originally published in Spanish as *Boca de lobo* by Alfaguara, 2000

First edition, 2013

Library of Congress Cataloging-in-Publication Data:

Chejfec, Sergio.
   [Boca de lobo. English]
   The dark / by Sergio Chejfec ; Translated from the Spanish by
   Heather Cleary. — First Edition.
      pages cm
   "Originally published in Argentina as Boca de lobo."
   ISBN-13: 978-1-934824-43-6 (pbk. : alk. paper)
   ISBN-10: 1-934824-43-7 (pbk. : alk. paper)
   I. Title.
   PQ7798.13.H38B613 2013
   863'.64—dc23
                                 2013010622

Printed on acid-free paper in the United States of America.

Text set in Fournier, a typeface designed by Pierre Simon Fournier (1712–1768),
a French punch-cutter, typefounder, and typographic theoretician.

Design by N. J. Furl

Open Letter is the University of Rochester's nonprofit, literary translation press:
Lattimore Hall 411, Box 270082, Rochester, NY 14627

www.openletterbooks.org

The
Dark

It has always unsettled me that geography does not change with time, with the changes that take place within it, within us. We retain something immaterial, similar to that something retained by geography, also immaterial. And yet, though it remains unaltered, geography is the measure of change. Just as happens with the temperature of a body, the trace it retains of its former heat allows it to continue being itself, yet this trace marks a difference. Bodies are and are not; they are at once more and less than. The same is true of geography, that is, it's unruly. I've read many novels in which the protagonist returns to a forgotten place. It doesn't matter whether the landscape is urban or rural. The slope of the hills won't have changed, but the green will be different, or the mountains, if they've kept their color, will disappoint with domesticated angles, not nearly as steep as remembered. The same goes for the city: the old corner has been restored, destroyed, abandoned, and so on. The protagonist is left with a residue, a mixture of reality and oblivion, something elusive drawn from his surroundings, the contradictory signs of which, along with his disappointment and resolve, allow him to recognize places. And so some characters, in order to uncover what lies hidden, latch on to the superficial.

This is exactly what is happening to me now. I go back to where I used to meet Delia and see that much has changed, while remaining

3

in place. This warehouse used to be an empty lot half a block wide where wildflowers would grow unchecked, floating lazily on a sea of thistles. Delia would tell me how the lot, also known as the thistle barrens, used to give her nightmares, before we—she, with her childhood barely behind her, and I, eager for her to forget it all the more quickly—pressed ourselves against the brick wall that surrounded it. The streets around there were gently sloped, and the buildings, I remember, gave the impression of having been constructed at random. Large industrial compounds bordered houses just over fifteen feet high, arranged in rows but crammed together— here the lines grew irregular, congested—to make the most of the elevation. The opposite was also true: a steel shed, no more than a large room, housed a factory with day and night shifts while, further off, a solitary residence rose up in the middle of a sprawling lot and was swallowed by the expanse. And yet, differences in size seemed irrelevant to Delia and me, as did spatial relations. Even the idea of "place" was called into question by our daily routine. There were no places, no confines; space was neither empty, nor full. Immune to all influence, nothing could contain us. The work of ages that defines the city, even the newer parts, did not exist to us. Distinctions were blurred; on our walks we could sense unfinished business, something just constructed or about to be abandoned, like a campsite taken down in a rush, something peaceful, rural and undefined that nevertheless seemed more lasting than the land itself. The solitude of the streets would attract distant sounds. For example, we would continue to hear the bus that had just left the corner of Los Huér-fanos after letting Delia off, though it was headed in the opposite direction and kept moving further from us. But a place could be absent or effaced and still be sensed by some part of ourselves, in our bodies, perhaps: as we neared the thistle barrens, Delia would begin

4

to sweat, almost imperceptibly. The sheen transformed her face, now paler than before, and turned her hands and arms to ice. She would tremble, youthful fear and adult desire joined in her agitation. Although attraction and resistance were no longer in opposition, she retained the memory of both, and the struggle between these recollections pushed her toward the brink. And so she got confused, not as a result of ignorance, inconsistency, or insecurity, but because she instinctively sensed that things on a threshold tend to remain incomplete. And Delia lived on a threshold: on the psychological border of her youth, and the physical one of her family.

It all began on the corner of Los Huérfanos, where I would watch her get off the bus. Delia would arrive as evening fell, place one foot on the pavement, and head straight for her house. Later on, I'll say more about the way she took that first step. I remember that someone would eventually turn up to wait for her. A woman would appear ten minutes before the bus and look down the road, intent on its arrival. Sometimes her impatience would show; she would clench her fists until they were red and fleshy, her hands eager to be doing something else. She'd greet Delia brusquely, take her arm, and the two of them would leave the corner and head down a side street. I always watched her get off the bus—the same foot, the same movement, the same air—until one day, by chance, I found out where she got on, and this meant guessing her occupation. The truth is, I don't remember the day or the circumstances, but I know that it happened like this: I was taking the bus in the opposite direction and saw someone standing just ahead with one arm raised. I recognized her back, her neck, her fingertips, the outline of her childish form carved out against the fading afternoon light. A few blocks to the east there was a school, a small, dilapidated structure that had been

5

there for a hundred years. Surely Delia was a student there. All of the town's battered pride converged on this school: there wasn't an older or more distinguished building around, and none was better suited to facing, by virtue of its presence alone, the pervasive feeling of adversity. Today, for example, I walked past and saw that it hasn't changed at all. At the appointed hours, students would spill from its doors and onto the streets, hungry and unaware of the deeper meaning, if there was one, of their routine. The girl who was Delia, at the time still nameless to me, presumably went into that building every day to, as they say, acquire knowledge. Then she would leave and begin the journey home, the culmination of which I knew well: the moment she stepped down onto the pavement on the corner of Los Huérfanos. The school radiated students, and Delia was one of its innumerable rays. Part of this routine was that the students would circulate aimlessly, carefree and unselfconscious, though everyone else was quite conscious of them. But unwanted knowledge often comes to us, anyway. I forgot in that first moment that just two blocks in the other direction, to the west, there was a factory. Unlike the school, the factory could go unnoticed by someone who didn't want to see it, and yet the truth lay there, and I'm not just talking about Delia. I mean that power emanated from the factory, authority; something at once imposing and caustic.

I disliked the fact that Delia worked, but it was an idea that had no clear shape. Contrary to what one might think, it was not a sentimental qualm or a matter of denouncing an injustice, at least, not in that sense. I disliked the fact that Delia worked for the most obvious of reasons; paradoxically, for the very circumstance that made her do so: because it turned her into something else, something outside herself, setting her feet on yet another border. Delia was probably no less innocent, if one can speak of innocence, than was normal for someone like her, but she did have different habits, a different routine. At any rate, she probably "knew" more, and different, things than other people her age. What she knew was what we don't want to know, but is, just the same. Still, later on, when we would spend nights walking along deserted streets, I felt a certain pride to know that the hands that sometimes touched me were the same ones that, hours earlier, had been operating machinery, handling tools, or moving future merchandise. These activities, designed primarily to make use of her physical strength—and, in the end, to sap it entirely— nonetheless granted her an immense vigor, in the form of an abundance or zeal that could overcome great adversity and moments of misfortune. Every so often I would think of the circle Delia represented: from the innocence I attributed to her at the beginning, to the strength of character one imagines the working class to have, then back to the simplicity of someone who considers her work to be essentially individual, so subjective it is invisible even to her. Delia was like that. This conviction could, in fact, have been grounded in profound wisdom, but it manifested itself in such a straightforward and constant way that it closed the circle perfectly, connecting the experiences and the sojourns of her spirit. The discovery that she worked in a factory, though it surprised me, was what made me fall in love with her. I can say, without exaggeration, that it was the mark that distinguished her from the rest of the human race, the condition that made her stand out from all other women. "Look at her . . . and a factory worker, at that . . ." I would think, assigning her a double density. As a thought it was empty, almost meaningless, but its shortcomings were compensated by the eloquence of the word and the circumstance: "worker." A silvery ring seemed to surround her, announcing her condition and emphasizing it among

7

other occupations and the titles these carry with them. And so each of her movements, even the mechanical one of stepping down with her right foot onto the corner of Los Huérfanos, took on another meaning. Although I didn't know her—she and I had never actually exchanged words, nor had I ever had the chance to observe her carefully, up close—Delia already embodied the most desirable, the most complete ideal of a woman. In this fragmentary, accidental way, all my senses were focused on her, trying at first to get their bearings as they received the signs of her movements each afternoon. When they finally achieved this, evidently, it was forever.

During our walks, Delia would ask how I really felt about her. Accustomed to the world of the factory, where truth is measured, counted, and classified, she was confused by the thought of becoming the object of something at once definite and intangible, as emotions tend to be. Because everything that can be counted is untrue. To confuse her further still, and to show her the absurdity of her misgivings, I told her that my words might be untrue but our experiences together were real; or, the other way around, that truthful words were driving us toward false actions. What I meant was that truth and falsity were terms that had no place in our world. How was Delia's way of thinking, which relied on accumulation and modification to measure change, distinct from that of a merchant, whose work is defined by the notion of difference? As a worker, Delia was in direct contact with the results of her labor: something was altered, a commodity was produced, or a piece was moved one step closer to completion. The merchant's way of thinking was different, being based on a change in category rather than a change in condition. In any event, Delia didn't own the things that passed through her hands, so her idea of measurability and concreteness was less calculated. As a worker, her position relative to these objects was at once subaltern and essential. The commodity determined her identity, it defined her as a worker; that same commodity also took her over, setting her apart by immeasurable distances as though she were from another world. Like geography, this movement is static, though this may seem contradictory: its meaning does not lie in change or circulation, in the idea of progress or a final objective, but rather in a movement that itself confers identity, like hours passing or, more appropriately, like those industrial pistons that do nothing but move back and forth. Delia's hands, then, were the surface upon which production attained the status of a commodity. I've read many novels in which the protagonist can't tell the difference between what is true and what is false—there is truth and falsehood in all things: people have true and false sides; someone chooses one part of a room as false and the other as true, and so on. I've even read an untrue book, or rather, a book falsified by circumstance, which described events that could have been real but eventually proved not to be. These events were both black and white; that is, they were neither. They were either outrageously false, or outrageously true. But with Delia, I was able to prove that these confusions meant nothing. Though she was sometimes at a loss for words, her expression was always appropriate, and no hint of ambiguity clouded her behavior. Coming from her, silence was something living, eloquent   it seemed crafted with the patience of stones, able to reveal the obvious without naming it.

One night, instead of walking around the Barrens, we crossed through them. Delia and I headed toward a house, a shack that bordered the street on the far side of the lot and in which reverberated the murmur of open spaces and unobstructed silence. We opened the door and the echo reached us before we set foot inside. It was the same as we walked in: the sound of each step bounced off the walls and returned to us before we had time to take the next one. Once more, without trying to, I was able to distinguish Delia's scent, which came to me mixed with those of the vegetation that surrounded us beyond the makeshift walls. Just as we had heard our footsteps before taking them, Delia's scent reached me as a premonition: I sensed it before my body was, as they say, joined to hers. In that moment, something was interrupted: time stood still, unable to contain what was happening. A jumble of scents, at times sharp and enigmatic, at times elusive, emanated from her. Later, I suppose, I'll describe Delia's scent, that invisible insignia, which in her case tended to fold in on itself and withdraw toward the greatest depths. Delia was timid, but never indecisive; her restraint was an indirect form of resoluteness, a deferral. The way she looked at me always unsettled me; her gaze was steady, true, and expressed itself only in terms of its depth, like wells do. What at first appeared to be caution was, in Delia, assurance, and what I interpreted as inhibition she experienced as desires that threatened and confused her in ways similar only in their urgency. What I mean is that Delia did not understand her desire—she was aware of it only as an assortment of vague ideas that she, nonetheless, was forced to obey as it pursued its own fulfillment.

I remember how we crossed the terrain. From the thicket of the night we stepped into another realm, thicker still: the Barrens, through which we haltingly felt our way, using our feet like hands. I walked ahead of Delia. The scents and vapors followed their individual paths, approaching one another, meeting and intermingling, showing that nature was still at its continuous, indolent work. Every so often a leaf would brush against our skin, leaving a slight irritation that burned when it came into contact with the air. Had we paused in that moment to examine our own actions, we wouldn't have known how to explain them: though it may be hard to believe, we were driven by instinct, not will, and certainly not conscience. It was as though I were being propelled by the same force that pressed the scents around us upward, something that gave the impression of being natural and abstract, but which nevertheless was directed toward a decisive end; at the same time, I could feel Delia pulling me along, even though she was behind me. Once inside the shack, we felt the walls recede. It was not my mouth that kissed her, not her hands that clutched at me. I looked at her without eyes and touched her without fingers. And that wasn't all: just as the memory of my hands on her breasts is the memory of my hands holding up the world, so too were the lips that kissed her not my own, but those of someone to whom I was joined, someone who surpassed me in every possible way, and under whose control I was given access to an abundance I would never have had otherwise. Delia's breasts were delicate and, obviously, small. I remember the sense of intoxication that came over me as I held them, those times they pointed downward, feeling the seed of her nipple in the center of my palm; I had only to lift them to be reminded of how absurdly light they were, like petals. Before stepping inside, Delia had begun to tremble. "It's the cold, the night air," she lied. At first I was taken aback, but immediately told myself that if Delia lied, then so must the night, the dew, the stars, and the thistles. A unanimous lie turned into truth. I remember the afternoon I first approached her; before saying a word, Delia looked at me in a way that suggested her response, not in words, but through her disposition. It said something like, "I am completely attentive to whatever you might say, and am determined to respond sincerely." Her eyes made this promise. She had barely stepped onto the corner of Los Huérfanos when I approached her and she met me in the way

11

I just described, with her transparent gaze. I, who already knew her secret, thought to myself that only a worker could respond that way. The proof of Delia's earnestness was precisely this: the fact that she was answering me before a question was ever asked.

Earlier, I mentioned the way she would set her foot on the pavement as she got off the bus. Now I'll describe it: it was like that of someone who spends their life crossing thresholds. The steps on buses, factory gates, the space between cobblestones, fences, doorways, the edge of a path. In her lightness, Delia never seemed able to access the memories she had so carefully gathered; she was there, but she gave the impression of having taken a long time to arrive. I said something above about a psychological border; it's basically the same thing. Watching her at her workstation, her concentration was obvious, and yet she handled the pieces with a distant, withdrawn air. She situated herself either in a before or an after, but never in that exact moment. The part of the factory to which Delia was most drawn was, precisely, its edge: the perimeter where discarded materials were scattered across the sparse and neglected grass, and where the weary curve of the fence still served as a boundary. The workers would go out there during their breaks to enjoy the space, in search of some distraction. Delia didn't need to be out there to appreciate it: long before the whistle sounded, she had already mentally taken her place on a large metal crate covered by a brown mat. On sunny days, four or five workers would climb up onto it. The holes in the mat, worn by time, allowed glimpses of the cold shine of metal that had once been meant for another purpose. Delia would start at the crate's lowest point and work her way up to the highest, conquering the slope. She would picture this before the whistle blew; it was what she did when she drifted off. She'd roll down her sleeves and, thus prepared for the outdoors, head for the perimeter, from where she would look out over the thick, high walls of the workshops that reflected the light like mountains. The slat windows that looked so small from outside filled the interior, as she well knew, with a harsh light, like powerful little suns. As might be expected, the grass grew thicker alongside the crate; as she sat, Delia would dangle her feet among the weeds.

Of all the novels I have read, I can't recall a single one that has taken the side of truth; at most, a few of them manage to uncover the trace of something concrete, definitive, but this is like the tip of an iceberg, hinting at all it conceals. The hidden part is a secret, or a threat that hangs over mariners. The same is true of names. Ships sail blindly through a night rife with danger, never knowing the risks hidden beneath the surface. I remember reading, once, about a crossing during which no one slept for a week. In the same way, I say "Delia" now and am overcome; I cannot speak her name, yet little happens when I write it. Writing is one thing, speaking, another. I remember the murmur, impossible to capture with words: "Delia, my Delia, it's me." The strokes required to trace out those five letters don't compare with the fleeting whisper, the fraction of a breath it took to say her name. Writing just one name or word involves a tremendous balancing act in which complex mental, motor, and visual operations come into play: an effort far greater than is required to pronounce them. In part because the written word is meant to endure. And yet we are weakest when faced with the temporary, with something whispered, spoken. Now, for example, when I say "Delia" under my breath, I tremble at the invocation because when I hear my own voice I feel as though I were calling her, or talking with her as I did years ago, as though she were just about to turn her attention to

13

me. I am left defenseless. What I mean to say is that there is more to Delia than just the woman, the worker, the person without whom I was unable to wake or to function; there are also the symbols and the forces hidden within her name. It may sound a bit esoteric, but that's how it is.

Heading north, the corner after Los Huérfanos was Pedrera. Delia and I rarely went that way, even though, as everyone who hung around Los Huérfanos knew, that was precisely where I came from; not exactly from that corner, but from that general direction. It's strange how ambiguous places and bearings can be. Pedrera wasn't the border of anything, and yet it was the start of something that actually began several blocks later, a fanning out of streets with no other name than just "past Pedrera," as it was called. To the inconclusiveness of place, then, was added the ambiguity of names: why should it be called "past Pedrera" if there were other streets with names of their own closer to—and therefore better suited to describing—what was "past" them? As I said, Delia and I almost never went in that direction, even though that was where I came from every afternoon and where I returned in the dark, in the small hours of the morning, her touch still fresh in my mind. The pressure Delia applied with her hands was something inhuman, even supernatural. It was the right and proper amount of pressure, at once premeditated and innocent, and I'm not just talking about her caresses. Delia's touch left a memory on the skin that would last for hours, and even then would only appear to fade: it might return as its reflection, an imagined graze of the fingertips that would leave one disoriented and defenseless because, in spite of its concrete origin, Delia, it could travel block after block through the darkness. These reflected touches manifested as a slight burn, like the sensation caused by contact with a thistle, and were concentrated around things that were, at that moment, intangible—the tautness of Delia's skin, the heat emanating from her body, the agitation caused by having her near—as though they were part of some gravitational field intent on testing its strength. And so, what I had felt as a pressure that, let's say, began with or was born of her hands, became, in her absence, the pressure exuded by the memory of her touch. Perhaps because of her age, Delia's pores breathed more than average. Her skin was dewy; it consoled and protected, but there was also something disconcerting about it. This is why I wrote earlier that I thought she was supernatural, because it felt as though I were touching an inscrutable surface that was neither smooth nor rough, nor was it opaque, translucent, or glistening. As with other mysteries from which one can only retreat, it never occurred to me to ask her about the strange quality of her skin. This confirms, I think, her enigmatic nature, though it also speaks to her utter simplicity, which presented itself as categorically as truth.

Delia was someone who never needed to be asked anything because she took it upon herself to respond before anything was said. I'm obviously talking about a certain kind of question, since some can only be asked and answered with words. There are those who think that the essential, precisely because it is so fundamental, can remain unspoken; that words attach themselves to and distort the truth. On the other hand, I've read many novels in which words are capable of revealing all, first hiding the truth under different layers of meaning, then revealing it the way the layers of an onion protect its core. And yet, when we get to the center, we find that there's nothing there, that the work of the onion was to justify itself and, in so doing, create itself. Are human lives just as useless and as self-contained?

That's what novels ask. Delia was both a promise and the fulfillment of that promise. She occupied a neutral territory. The first time she asked me to do something for her, I noticed her tendency to disappear, to dissolve among people and things, leaving apparently incidental traces behind her in what is known as the day-to-day world, the indifferent witness to her movements and actions. I may return to this idea later, this double inclination of Delia's: to disperse and distribute parts of herself while remaining distant, contracting and expanding at once.

For a long time, as I said, we would take the same route every night through the thistle barrens and the surrounding area. One evening, though, Delia wanted to make a detour and asked me if I wouldn't mind going a few blocks further with her. Given how I felt at the time—how I still feel—I said of course, anything, whatever she wanted. Delia explained that she had to pick up some clothes. We didn't head toward Pedrera, or toward her place; we went to a neighborhood full of half-built houses inside which packs of children played. At night it was hard to tell if the structures were ruins, or if something was being built there: a neighborhood, a settlement, a community, individual houses, and so on. That's what I thought—or what Delia and I thought—at the time; now I don't think there's much of a difference. Everything built is the promise of a future ruin, even new constructions. We live surrounded by debris; living in a house means inhabiting a ruin—and I don't mean this only in a literal sense. The children's arms and faces could be seen through the holes left for windows; sometimes they would try, unsuccessfully, to hide behind the thin concrete columns that held nothing up. I remember those faces, lit by the moon, furtive like the animals. Never before had a place seemed so entirely left to the mercy of

God, though I had seen worse. It was the sense of incompletion, the feeling that nature neither offered resistance—because no one had challenged it—nor made any demands; it wanted only to affirm its presence in the face of the man-made world. We walked in silence for more than an hour; the night passed while the landscape stayed the same. Though impossible, this happened as if it were true. And this was because we belonged to a misleading order of things: it was not that the landscape didn't change, but rather that it didn't matter to Delia or to me. My "landscape" was at my side: it was her, a face that presented itself for contemplation freely and without discomfort, partly confident and partly indifferent to those who fixed their attention on it. Just as the wind suggests the activity of the world by stirring the leaves, the breeze that ran through Delia's hair exhibited her concentration, which I'd almost describe as a withdrawal, a surrender unique in that she was not giving up anything in particular. These waves, the work of the wind in her hair, were yet another sign of how entirely fitting her presence was. As in a classical image, depth and mystery emanated from this movement, yet it was a contradictory sort of mystery because it relied on a superficial instrument like the air to manifest itself. In the same way, just like at work, Delia surrendered a part of herself when she withdrew; someone observing her might think that at any moment she might cease to be herself, that she might succumb to a force that would isolate and take over her body. But something kept her from crossing that threshold, and this was how Delia was able to maintain the delicate balance between absence and communion.

I said before that the landscape mattered little, that my landscape was the one I kept at my side: her. I experienced that long string of ruins—ex-houses or pre-buildings, scattered across the terrain and indifferent to the way people used them—as a kind of delay or postponement, something secondary to what happened in real life, in the true landscape. But what was Delia's landscape? I was at her side, therefore it was me. This may sound rash, and maybe a bit vain, but I don't have any memories that would contradict it—much less from that night. In many novels a character's nature manifests itself through his face; a portrait is read, a soul glimpsed. But the truth is that faces speak of themselves and also of varied, even contradictory things; they never indicate one thing alone. A serene neck tenses suddenly and for no apparent reason; what can be read into this, aside from the anxiety of the observer? The confusion of the person to whom the gesture was directed? A sensual lip twitches not with desire, but disdain; the arch of a forehead promises intelligence, but also hints at the betrayal soon to follow. Sparkling eyes, as big as moons and as deep with sincerity as the wells I mentioned earlier when speaking of Delia, offer themselves up and crumble, emptied out without ever giving what they promised. An imploring brow, innocent cheeks, nostrils flared with passion. And yet faces say the opposite, contradicting their individual parts. The strength that Delia transmitted, that serene focus, was concentrated in her eyebrows. They were thick and bushy, and though they belonged to something as conventional as a face might seem to be, they were the mark of an untamed or savage past; a sign that became a promise that was, nonetheless, fulfilled.

I had been mistaken about the phrase "pick up some clothes," the same way I had been about what I'd wanted to see and not to see when I discovered where Delia caught the bus. "Picking up some clothes" meant, to me, "picking up some clothes I lent someone." This was evidently a specific reading, not exactly wrong, but incorrect.

It was also less straightforward than the one I had not wanted to imagine, but which was true all the same: that Delia needed to borrow clothes because there were times when she had nothing else to wear. I discovered this a few days later, under sad circumstances, when she had to return what she'd borrowed. We were walking along a dirt road. It had rained the day before, and as the earth dried out, the steam that rose from the puddles smelled of mud, a scent that called to mind roots, leaves, fruit, and animals or insects, all mixed together. The smell was strong, unmistakable; it felt like being within centimeters of the ground, to that height just above the surface where the particles float at the mercy of the air, the weather, and the movements of the earth, which lift them and then let them fall again, forming a crust in a state of permanent suspension, a halo of proximate gravity. Anyway: we were walking along, upright, as saturated with the humid scent of the mud as if we had been close enough to taste it, when Delia suddenly said, "I hope a car doesn't splash me, I have to return this skirt tomorrow." The skirt was dark, blue or black, depending on the light. I had been reflecting on the skirt all along, since I noticed that it made Delia's hips, so attractive in their innocence and the harmony of their shape, more attractive still. As she walked, her legs seemed to be holding up a mystery, a bud waiting for the right moment to burst open and unfurl. What I mean is that the skirt seemed to have been made for Delia, that its essence or meaning was only fully realized when, as is always said of the primary function of attire, it shielded her from the elements. But this impression crumbled as soon as I heard her remark. It took me a while to understand that such loans could belong to an order as natural as any other—possession, for example; the idea that the skirt had been made especially for Delia was no less true because she could only wear it when it had been lent to her. This gave the loan

19

a new significance: it was the alias fate had chosen to reveal a truth, in this case one that involved Delia, which otherwise would have remained hidden.

That afternoon, I also discovered that the concept of a loan might encompass different, even contradictory, meanings. A loan, a debt. I've read several novels that try to determine the meaning of these words. I don't know if they succeed; in any event, none present a model of loans or debt that resembled the way Delia seemed to see them. Delia believed that a loan could never be repaid in full, that the loan itself brought about a decisive change in the general course of events, and therefore that the idea that giving something back was a repayment, compensation, or a return to normal was misguided and incomplete. She believed that the loan remained active over time, even after it was paid back. This was because the object, in this case a skirt, retained traces of its various owners, or rather, of the various people who had used it over time. These marks, which made the objects unique and unmistakable, were invisible to the average person yet were indelible in the eyes of the community. With each new loan, the collective appreciation of the object—here, the skirt—grew. The article of clothing itself could deteriorate with use and circulation, but this damage was mitigated by the greater care everyone would take of it. As such, time limits were rarely imposed on these loans. Not because there was no pressure to return the item, but because, since the object was marked by each custody, the debt was reproduced in the memory of the community. That was debt, according to Delia: a repayment that was both unnecessary and always deferred. It was clearly a definition far removed from material concerns, at least, as these are generally understood. And this in spite of the fact that she lived, as perhaps I'll describe later, with the daily reminders of that other, broader type of loan, the kind geared toward profit. It's true that even before that moment, it had been obvious that the skirt could not have belonged to Delia; still, my surprise when I discovered it wasn't hers was an effect of that part of the obvious we don't want to acknowledge. The obvious side of things seems innocent, insubstantial, there for the sole purpose of holding up the hidden face of what is not obvious. And yet, the world organizes itself according to what is revealed. In this way, Delia's comment about the loan added a measure of truth to what was already evident, and the weight of this reality became more pronounced.

I saw her several times in her uniform when she went out to what the workers called the yard, the perimeter around the factory where the patchy grass was a surreal shade of gray. I'd watch Delia from the other side of the wire fence during her afternoon break: always wearing the same nondescript clothes in the same drab color, sometimes sitting on the crate. Like the clothing of her fellow workers, Delia's was inseparable from what it represented, from the function it served, had served, and would always serve. A kind of nakedness manifested itself through these clothes. A nakedness that made the skin seem useless, inexpressive. I watched her cohort: a gray, formless mass among which Delia was a twinkling star, a light on the verge of being absorbed, or of breaking free in the form of its own miniature. Workers gathered during the break, silent and barely moving. I remember them looking resigned, dressed in the same color and covered by a shadow that moved over them slowly, like a cloud. That mix of shadow and light, an effect that at first appeared random, but which followed a mysterious order, was the only noticeable movement. There was nothing to be revealed there, apart from the hum of the group, the glimmer of Delia, and the factory's imposing presence.

A few of the workers had their own habits and customs; still, I don't think I would be doing them any great injustice if I said they behaved like a herd. They kept to the furthest corner of the yard, reached by a worn dirt path. Even the short break the factory allowed them was long enough to make them restless; one could sense their discomfort, the impatience that united them, but against which they also needed to defend themselves. As Delia once explained to me, this was because they spent most of their time in the factory, focused on their machines, surrounded by the metal particles that floated in the air and that constant, loud clanging. And yet, I thought as I observed Delia and her fellow workers from outside the fence that surrounded the factory, what would under different circumstances mean standing out—doing something unusual, stepping outside one's habitual environs—was precisely what made them nebulous, what reduced them. From a distance, they seemed to withdraw into themselves, huddled together against the surrounding expanse. This amorphousness united them, underscored their status as part of a group rather than as people. There is an expression, which is perhaps a bit harsh and also fairly ambiguous, but is illustrative in this case: "collective body." That is, not something connected with institutions or hierarchies, like a labor union in a factory, but rather a being made up of numerous identical individuals with a molecular life of its own. Some of the workers moved in orbits around the rest, others followed a more complex trajectory, passing in front of some and behind others without a clearly defined course. Then there were the individual movements: someone would lower his head, rest his hands on his hips or shoulders, and so on. In any event, the observer was witness to an unclear and vaguely theatrical scene, in which the gray uniforms of the workers, distorted by variations in the light, fused the movements of the group and revealed them as mere concentrations of color and depth.

I would be standing at a distance from them, on the other side of the fence—today that wire mesh has become a dense, solid grille—or even on the other side of the street, in fact, and notice that I was not the only one transfixed by the scene. Little by little, the corner filled with people who stood watching the formless tribe and its smooth, controlled movements, just as I did. I think the sensation of witnessing a special kind of ceremony—in this case, the rudiments of a rite celebrating idleness; a scene that unfolds only insofar as it is observed, that has neither beginning nor end, but rather has the steady temperament of animals, undistracted and uninterrupted—I think this sensation of confronting an excess of nature derived in large measure from their attire. Fat or thin, tall or short, the whole group wore its uniform like a second skin. I'll talk later about the connection the workers had to this second skin, about the cruel paradox it inflicted upon them when they had to choose between saving themselves and remaining themselves. For now I'll just say that the uniforms collectively evoked the most obvious thing, that is, the clothing of prisoners and so on; on another level, though, repeated across the bodies of Delia and her peers, creating the play of light and movement I described earlier, they produced a different effect: a sense of exaggerated volume, a mass, like a topographical feature that had emerged out of nowhere.

Delia stood out in this anonymous, yet paradigmatic, scene. Things took on a greater value with her; if there was a general air of indifference, she was the most indifferent of all, and where there was grace to be found, it obviously came from the most graceful person present: Delia. She moved among the rest like one more member of the family, but also like someone who knows she's one of the chosen few. In this case, the distinction was even greater, because she was also "my" chosen one. Through her clothing, Delia showed signs of the work she did in the factory. And though sometimes these marks made me think she did work unsuited to a body like hers, I should say that, at other times, I felt a vague sense of satisfaction—something between pride and compassion—at the wounds that appeared on her second skin. When the whistle sounded and Delia rolled down her sleeves to go out to the yard, the part that covered her forearms revealed the shirt's former appearance. In the contrast between the protected and the exposed fabric, one could imagine the time she spent at the machines. This was one way of knowing what went on inside the factory, one way of glimpsing that hidden truth. We can read or hear about life in a factory, learn about the work that's done there, the processes that are carried out, the rules that are followed, and so on, but the fact that we receive each new detail greedily, always hungry for more, is proof of how little we really know. In that same way, I pored over Delia's uniform when she lowered her sleeves: I wanted to find the detail, the accidental mark that, together with clues I had received earlier, would allow me to reconstruct her shift. Clothes are particularly good for this, aren't they? I've read many novels in which characters study the clothing of others to learn something about them, something their words don't say and their actions don't reveal. There are even novels in which someone is fooled by clothing, though they know it to be a prime form of trickery. This was not the case with Delia. Much is written about the accessory, but very little about the essential. Earlier I said that when the workers gathered in the yard, the light reflecting off their worn clothes was like that of a cloud blanketing the sky and covering the bodies below with the fleeting memory of ash. Well, I was wrong: it was actually that their silhouettes were suspended in a translucent liquid, as though enveloped by a shadow projected from the ground. The movements of this reflected light deformed their bodies, and yet one could also say it gave them life, in that it was these variations that made them visible. Put like this, I'm not sure the metaphor reveals anything; still, there is little to reveal. One doesn't write to uncover what is hidden, but rather to obscure it further. If that is what I'm doing now, it is because everything about Delia and all the rest of it speaks for itself with absolute clarity; given the eloquence of the events themselves, I can fall silent.

I remember one afternoon, they saw me from the yard. The sun hit the ground with a sudden and tremendous force, discrediting the millions of miles that separated one from the other. My thoughts wandered between the workers and our distance from the sun; I got distracted by ideas of a basic symbolism, like the paradox that, since all the energy in nature is derived from the sun, the workers embodied a power that holds reality up and drives it forward. The group acknowledged me, not as Delia's boyfriend, but rather as a passer-by—they had to call me something—straining to see them, whose attitude fell somewhere between admiration and shock. The observer dreams of being anonymous, as everyone does. I felt exposed when they noticed me; for a moment it seemed as though their clothes were no longer the reflection of something else. Something told me there was no reproach in their silence, and that they were willing to do whatever was necessary—if they were called upon and knew what to do—to ensure that my contemplation of them would not be interrupted. No one looking in from the outside would have noticed anything unusual, and the truth is that nothing unusual was going on. Though the sum of its parts confirmed that this was, in fact, what I was seeing, the slightest disruption of any detail could have changed the situation entirely. For example, it could have been a party out in the country, with farmhands about to down their umpteenth drink while the country girls breathed in their desire, as they had already been doing for some time. But the group of workers was more than the sum of its parts; embedded within it were the elements that I, summoned for no apparent reason and with little enthusiasm to this factory rite, had added. At some point it occurred to me that they were waiting for me to decide the show was over, turn, and continue on my way. Just as I had invented them as a herd or a choreographed troupe, as an object to be observed and examined, I would imagine their existence had come to an end, like someone getting up to shut off a television set. Of all the different kinds of uniform, that of a worker is the most necessary, the most natural. I've seen people become workers the moment they put on that uniform for the first time. And so Delia, I said to myself, was one of them. I mentioned her uniform earlier, calling it her second skin, the garment that allowed a deeper essence to show through. Now it seems more like a first, rather than a second, skin; that there was more truth in the clothing than in the skin itself.

Delia was worried that a car might splash mud on her skirt, though it was obvious that it would be days before a car passed through there. That street typically didn't see traffic for weeks at a time; the tracks left by the vehicles gradually wore away, leaving behind shallow grooves where water collected, a record of the infrequent transit. We got to the house where Delia was supposed to return the skirt, isolated in the middle of what was theoretically a block, though it had no visible borders. The lots were marked by wire, dilapidated fences, or piles of stones and broken cinderblocks meant to suggest walls. There were no other structures, though I have a memory of walking along a corridor. There were no trees, either, just a few prickly shrubs and a bit of grass that grew precariously between them. The narrow, winding path was a rift worn by footsteps headed toward the house, which rose from the middle of the vast lot as though it were the center of the universe. As we walked, I thought about the night and, obviously, the thistle barrens, remarking to myself that differences mean less in the dark. Creatures of the light, humans need to adjust themselves to the night. The little path that led to the house was like one you might find in a forest, but there were no trees to be seen; it seemed extravagant in its simplicity, gratuitous in that it crossed nothing worth crossing. The owner of the skirt, who needed it that night, was waiting at the other end. The house was a hovel; in this, too, it resembled the thistle barrens. Delia opened the door without knocking or saying a word, and we stepped into a large, empty room. Dirt floors, rickety furniture, scattered appliances spotted with rust that was a deeper red than the ground. I won't elaborate on the scene; I'll add only that the windows were holes with sharp and irregular borders punched out of the walls, the kind you see in a poorly cut piece of sheet metal. My mind turned to the house, the neighborhood, to the poor sort of poetry that emerged from them; it was a scene that at first glance appeared weak, worn, on the verge of collapse. At one point, Delia stepped out to get changed. She came back in an old pair of pants, which I recognized, with the skirt tucked under her arm. She wasn't gone long, no longer than it would take anyone to take off a skirt and put on a pair of pants, but it was long enough for me to think that the house—and not just the house, but the whole area—lacked both a past and a future. I could see traces of the labor of man, of the distracted signs of routine, the growth of a community, and so on; still, these were the marks of an invisible labor as accidental as that of nature. People working diligently, like ants, without a clear purpose and at the mercy of chance . . .

When Delia's friend stepped out a little while later to try on the skirt, or simply to put it on, I wondered whether we didn't pass through this world as anonymous beings, driven by a force at once innocent, merciless, and brutal. Delia felt protected from this power and, thanks to her condition—as a woman and a worker—resisted its influence. I have often thought that it is workers, with their bodies and the force they exert at the expense of their own energy, who atone for our indifference toward the world; that first, foremost, and in a literal sense, they pay out in labor what they receive as wages— an amount never equal to the true value of their efforts—but also that they pay for that which has no price, that is, for the infinite debt racked up by humanity. I was familiar with the operations whereby Delia's friend would take off her clothes and put on the skirt: universal maneuvers that, in this particular case, were meant to confirm that it still looked good on her, as they say. The friend was out there somewhere, barely protected from prying eyes by the walls of the shack, or in the narrow bathroom, where the absence of light could be misleading: mistaking darkness for size, one ended up banging one's feet and elbows against the walls. The kitchen was in one corner of the house; within its limited radius, a dense concentration of objects alluded to constant and, though it may seem contradictory, discontinuous actions. Delia was silent; she seemed to be thinking only of the imminent return of her friend. This was not exactly a thought, but it would be excessive to call it a premonition. We were taking part in one of the millions of micro-scenes that everyone enacts, all the time. The movement of the air could be heard, punctuated occasionally by drafts that whistled through the walls when the breeze picked up. At that moment there was little to say, so we didn't speak for a while. In one corner, a gas burner rested unstably on the cylinder that fed it, surrounded by a jumble of pots, pans, and jugs, each set in the exact spot dictated by its use; this space was the origin of the invisible thread that tied the home together. It was palpable: the heat that warmed milk for the little ones, food for the adults, and so on, extended throughout the home and the time that existed within it, leaving its indelible mark. It was the presence that, for example, would allow the blind child to know that this was the interior of his own home, where his family lived. The rest of the dwelling was in shadow, and though the darkness was similar to that of the kitchen, everything in it was harder to see, more confused; the tangle of blankets, mattresses and pieces of foam rubber thrown together at absurd angles, like fallen dominos, belonged—or seemed to follow—to a logic that differed from, or contradicted, that of the kitchen. Whereas the kitchen signified a concentrating force, the rest of the house suggested a force of diffusion. It was there that dreams and desires went about their work, the space, even, in which bodies tried to escape themselves. At that instant, the two orders stood at bay, coexisting in an unconditional peace; this was the resonance of the moment. One could picture two sleeping armies unaware of their own weakness, their own narcissism and, most of all, their respective opponents.

I'd had nothing to say earlier, either, when Delia went to take off the skirt and I found myself alone with her friend. She was almost certainly waiting for a platitude, some incidental remark (even if nothing I said could be described as such), but I felt that the person who united us, Delia, was also the line that divided us, a barrier that could not be crossed. The walls were more articulate: the corner where the kitchen stood, as dark and cluttered as a shrine, said more than the distracted silence of Delia's friend. It was into the hands of this transparent being that Delia would deposit that most delicate and flattering of skirts, I thought; the article of clothing that made her even more unique, that made her stand out to me as my chosen one and made the strongest case for the natural quality of her beauty. This could be understood as another of the paradoxes imposed on us by the notion of property: things don't always belong to the right person; aside from those who have very little, most people don't feel they have enough. They always want more, or different, things. I've read many novels that turn a blind eye toward property; characters come and go, or stay, forget one another, carry on. The same goes for actions. But this omission of property is a mistake, because the universe built around it is taken for granted as natural. This might have been a good topic for breaking the silence with Delia's friend, but I missed that opportunity as well. I have forgotten her name but still recall the image of her fingers playing with the hem of the shirt she wore that afternoon. It was green with little pictures of dried fruits, walnuts, chestnuts, and so on printed on it. When its owner's fingers closed around the fruits as though naïvely trying to pick them, they revealed the unexpected, though logical, justification of the pattern.

Though according to Delia they were the same age, her friend looked older. Like everyone else in that meager community, she had been born in the provinces. When she was still a girl, her mother's brother sent for her. Someone, she did not remember who, took her to the station to put her on a train. On the platform, she saw men smoking cigarettes that were remarkable for their whiteness. She had always been fascinated by the things with which men surrounded themselves. Whether these were handkerchiefs, key rings, or cigarettes, Delia's friend revered them in a way that was passing only insofar as it moved from one object to immediately settle on another. During the trip she watched someone smoke in an enclosed space for the first time, but what really startled her was the flash of something shiny one man held to his chest. He was sitting with his back to her at the other end of the car. To catch a glimpse of the metallic object without knowing what it was, to worship it as an element of the masculine, but not to recognize it: this threefold sensation multiplied her anxiety. The next morning the passenger took a swig from it and she discovered that it was a flask. Now she knew what the object was, but still wondered what its name could be. This renewed ignorance doubled the mystery and increased her fascination. For the rest of the trip she had thoughts, daydreams, like these; if there was something worth knowing it was these objects of men and the promise they held of lasting happiness, not the sad life out in the country. When the train arrived at its destination, Delia's friend readied herself to get off. She grabbed her bundle of clothes and her little suitcase, looked at her shoes, and paused. She felt she should prepare herself, that after so many days the moment had finally come. Though he had gone to meet her, her mother's brother hid when he saw her standing alone on the platform. She sensed a presence, the weight of a gaze upon her, but did not know where it was coming from. Her mother's brother never did reveal himself, but he went on observing her. He had no particular reason for doing this; his behavior was the product of a vague idea regarding family: that it was at once a lasting bond and a connection always on the verge of being lost. Because danger lies hidden where security takes root. And there is nothing more dangerous than a niece, thought the man. The girl stood on the platform until nightfall. There are many novels that say: One never stops waiting, though a lifetime may go by. She was already homesick; this was clear to her even though she was generally used to ignoring her feelings. But what kept her from turning back was the same force that had driven her forward and not, ultimately, the presence of her uncle, whom she imagined was still waiting for her. To her, waiting was a state that never ended. And so the two of us waited patiently for Delia to return, wearing her regular clothes, with the flattering skirt tucked under her arm.

Once accustomed to the smells inside the shack, one could make out the scent of the wilderness, or at least certain scents associated with something called the wild. From one direction came a moist, warm vapor heavy with sharp odors and unclassifiable particles; from another, the familiar smell of turned dirt, a combination—cold, in this case—of roots and stones that one immediately associated with darkness and depth. These smells were the only commonplace things there. What I mean is that they were the only things that indicated the presence of a known, familiar world. I could say, though the statement might seem a bit outrageous, that it was only because of these smells that I was in "my country." They made their way in and lingered, vanishing only when a new set of odors took their place. I've read many novels in which scents allow lost memories to be recovered, showing that stronger, truer connections reveal themselves when consciousness gives itself over to chance. But those novels don't talk about familiar smells, or rather, those of recent memory, the ones that appear more predictably than the sun to remind us of the circular patterns in which we are immersed. The smells in Delia's friend's house were neither one, nor the other; there was no truth behind them, just a few longstanding convictions that couldn't be sustained without outside intervention. As I've mentioned, a severed landscape could be seen through the window. No matter how idyllic they might be, the things beyond it forced their way through its jagged opening in little bites. We know the landscape never speaks with just one voice, and not only because no two gazes are alike. The window invited one to look outward; it was the element that made the house real. The inside of the house belonged to one dimension, the exterior to another. The precariousness of the window that separated the two spheres revealed the general sense of uncertainty. At that point, another episode in the life of Delia's friend came to mind, something that happened on the train that took her from her place of birth: as she thought devotedly about men's belongings, she was mistaken for someone else. (Delia's friend went over to one of the beds, produced a notebook and, opening it, showed me a photo in which she was younger, almost a child, and wore a restrained expression that concealed reserve and promised boldness.)

As she headed toward the unknown, she had to confront a greater, more complex, abstraction. A few hours before the episode, the train had stopped at a remote station. The platform was stone gray with a faded white border, the remnants of a coat of whitewash. The building gave the impression of being low to the ground; the shabbiness of its walls seemed to reduce its height. While she waited, Delia's friend had ample time to study the platform, which could only hold two cars. The sun set unimpeded, and the few trees that flanked the building caught no light. Their green was starting to fade; they've lost their strength, she thought. If someone had suddenly caught a glimpse of the scene they would have thought it had been staged: a girl standing at the window of a train car, looking out. Delia's friend was distracted by shapeless ideas that were replaced by others before they could be fully formed, or which returned unexpectedly after having been left incomplete. She thought, for example, about how the train's shadow disregards the tracks. The silhouette of the cars rests on the station floor, sketching out a step as it climbs the platform and continues, uninterrupted, before descending into the wild on the other side. This fact, the forceful contour of a shadow, left Delia's friend deep in thought for a long time. She sensed that nature tended to be arbitrary, but preferred to reveal itself with caution. Her experience back home had taught her this, and the events that followed—like the dull sun above her, the silence of the station—and the things around her—arranged precisely to appear and break her attention—only confirmed it. She thought: "It's not so bad, being alone," or something like that. She was looking out the window and repeating this idea until something startled her: someone was watching her from nearby. She felt she was in danger, but her fear quickly subsided. She was pleased that she had caught the eye of a stranger: at least one thing in this overwhelming, though static, situation was directed at her. Later, she would remember the man's steps as he approached, without being able to assign them any particular tempo: they were either innumerable or too few, but never the two things at once. She was confused, unsure what her reaction should be, when something else unsettled her even more: the stranger was carrying a small photo, from which he didn't lift his eyes. She thought she heard a noise, maybe they were hitching another car to the train. The man finally reached her and stood in silence. A silence that said little, but which had the unmistakable eloquence of anticipation.

Delia's friend didn't know what to do; from the window she could see the faint shadow of the car, the even line of the roof. Just like trains in stations, people leave traces on one another that almost immediately fade away. The thought appealed to her, since she wanted the man to be gone as quickly as possible. She suddenly remembered stories she'd heard; the people from her neighborhood, all of whom were poor, tended to believe in miraculous scenarios in which millionaires unexpectedly find a long-lost daughter living in anonymity and neglect. Her mind raced, it seemed impossible to focus on the urgent thoughts that filled it. The man finally spoke, though it was only to ask her name. Delia's friend did not know how to answer something so simple. All questions are difficult, but familiar ones are especially problematic. They involve an act of memory, like when an adult calculates his age based on what year it is. In the end, as she said her name, she realized—though she had been aware of this all along—that she was moving farther and farther from home. She knew that her response, though true, broke a bond that had been strong until that moment. The man, for his part, didn't believe what he'd heard; "It can't be," he said, as he turned the photo around so she could see it. Delia's friend grimaced. Her solitude had been ambushed at the flank where we are all most vulnerable. She saw her own image in the photo, recognized each of her features from the memory, for example, of her fingers touching her face. She repeated to herself that it was impossible, and wondered what the outcome of this adventure might be. In her innocence she thought that if she had lied, none of this would have happened, that the coincidence lay not between the image and her face, but between herself and her name. It should be said that the matter was never resolved. She immediately discovered a new problem that only made the situation worse: there was another difference, which, although it affected the physical resemblance, also emphasized it. The tone of their skin was not the same. Though this was obvious, the stranger did not notice. For Delia's friend, seeing herself with different skin meant being transported: not to a future or a past, but to a simultaneous, contiguous time.

Later, repeating the story in Delia's presence, the friend added that the photograph the man had been carrying was actually of a painting, an oval-shaped portrait with a dark background and a fake gold frame. What she had first imagined to be the photograph of a person, as true as a legal document, became a drawing that dissolved into an unimaginable series of mediations. A turn of the screw, she said in different words, that complicated things further still. Because if the evidentiary proof, as they say, was a painting, the model was less important than the hand that had given her form. It seemed that the artist, whether he was right or wrong, had created a patient prophecy: the encounter with the model would eventually take place; the time and distance that needed to be crossed before this occurred were secondary. And so the episode was fixed in Delia's friend's past against a backdrop of confusion. It could not be said that she had forgotten it, but the mystery, which still left her anxious and often on the verge of tears, was such that she did not want to remember.

After I abandoned her, the first news I got of Delia was that she'd had the child. For a while, as I may explain later, there had only been chance encounters. I might run into her anywhere, wherever she had gone looking for me. For me, who wanted to forget, coming face to face with her was always a surprise. Having waited for hours, Delia would sometimes get distracted and not see me coming; on those occasions, I could sneak away in time, before she realized. But sometimes she saw me before I'd noticed her and I had to make my escape without shame or compassion. I needed time to pass quickly and to break the spell of having her in my sight, so I did the first thing I could—cross the street, look away—I don't know, I tried to hide, though hiding was the most treacherous reaction possible. I knew there was nowhere to conceal myself: open to the point of exaggeration, vast and transparent, those flat expanses revealed even the indiscernible. But I tried, anyway. I don't know how Delia reacted; I mean, I'm not sure what effect my behavior had on her. She'd watch me take off, and probably couldn't understand it. I suppose the fact that the landscape kept me from hiding was yet another sentence passed down on her, because I was always in view. These encounters were brief, but they must have felt intolerably long to Delia. Things were no better for me; it was a pathetic sort of ending, and I knew deep down that none of these tricks would ever be enough. For example, I could jump behind some bushes or run away; Delia wouldn't follow me, but these were only ways of mitigating an irreparable situation, that is, the fact that she'd seen me, when what I really needed was to blend in, go unnoticed, disappear—all of which were inconceivable in those parts.

Another thing that house had was flies, which were more of a presence there than in most other places I've been. Delia's friend lifted a large pot to show it to me, and as I made out the dents on the bottom of it, the marks left by children tirelessly banging spoons against it, a fly emerged, startled, from the shadows. A common occurrence in people's lives, this took on a particular meaning there. It may seem a bit naïve, but I saw it as another indication of the boundless hospitality of the poor. I'm not ashamed to put it like that, leaving a number of other things out. They were fat, black flies that had been part of the household for a long time. Every so often one would waver and seem to be on the verge of falling mid-flight as though, suddenly and without any external or internal force having alerted it to the fact, the animal had just become aware of its own mass, and was shocked by it. As a result, it would fly quickly upwards. Delia's friend leaned over in the dark, looking for some other object to show me—a little later, she would find a tin with combs in it between two mattresses— when I suddenly wondered whether we might not all be flies as well. We submit ourselves to life just as they do, floating over the earth until we are startled by our own weight. It would have been hard to convey this to the lady of the house, I could imagine the uncomfortable silence she would offer in response, so it hardly seemed worth it, though it's not as though there were much to explain. While Delia was changing, I kept getting the impression that her friend was about to say something. Showing me things was her way of communicating; this became especially clear when it would take her a moment to find something new and she'd open her mouth as though she were about to speak, only to immediately change her mind.

Later, as we left the house, I got the impression that I was stepping into a world that was different somehow, enclosed. It should have been the other way around: one goes into a house to escape one's surroundings, but as I passed through the doorway I thought that the outside was actually the real inside, the true interior. Delia was beside me, quiet, exposed to the elements. The inside of the house felt like the outside, and the outside like the house, or rather, it felt like the house was an infinite expanse and its surroundings were only a part of the whole. We paused on the other side of the door where the ground dipped a bit, worn down from having been trod on so often. On either side, two flowerbeds sprouting different types of weeds indicated that someone, at some point, had wanted to plant a garden there, though they had almost certainly forgotten about it since. The immensity of the territory stretched out before us, an apparently limitless expanse flecked with clusters of shrubs, scattered houses, and gentle slopes. It wasn't just the size of the surface that gave this sensation: one saw it this way because of its homogeneity, the vertigo of simple things. This simplicity ennobled the landscape, but it also silenced it, deprived it of a voice. It was the house that spoke for it, the house that endowed it with meaning, an existence. The house behind us, the broad territory ahead. Something small that justified something large; it occurred to me that expansiveness is incidental when there is a center to it, and that center was behind us just then. The light was fading; soon it would be night.

As we made our way back, Delia told me a few things about her friend, specifically the details of what had happened on that legendary train ride. She described the monotony of its route; it had seemed like a journey into the depths that, as such, would never end. Delia told stories as though nothing in the world could distract her. She said that the man, seeing the girl's confusion, took a second portrait from his pocket, showed her that they were identical, and gave it to her. Before he left, he tousled her hair paternally. Delia's friend would spend the years that followed contemplating her double. The longer she spent with the image tucked among her clothes, the more at one with it she felt. Talisman, key, salvation. She set the portrait in the upper corner of her mirror and would draw near; wide-eyed, she searched for differences, eager to discover something that had gone unnoticed until that moment. The sessions were exhausting: the friend derived a deferred, circumspect pleasure from studying one face and then the other. Time passed, and she had little to show for it. She began asking herself, more and more frequently: How can one find something intangible? Accustomed to the workings of the mirror, reflection and portrait seemed the same to her, to the extent that, had her features not been identical to the model's, the habit of looking at them would have eventually made them seem so anyway. That is, the prevalence of ambiguity made difference and novelty impossible. Days passed, then months. In her cryptic manner, after a taxing but revelatory session, one day Delia's friend had a premonition: "From now on, finding something will never mean finding something new." It would be the other way around, she thought: discovering something old, something that had always been there, but had never been seen. This feeling of connection and frustration was the bond that joined her to the image. As Delia spoke, the path disappeared beneath our feet. Although we couldn't see it, the ground made itself known through its unevenness, catching us by surprise and making us stumble. The pitch-black night grew denser toward the edges of the street, where clumps of bushes, abandoned objects, and motionless animals attracted us with the pulse of their presence the way the current draws a swimmer off course. This blackness, which seemed strange and probably hostile, was precisely the opposite to us: it reminded us of the blackness of the Barrens. The dark, a stimulus that promised something intimate, untamed. Every now and then we'd see a flicker in the distance: someone carrying a light. Other times, a solitary streetlamp would illuminate the air, which was absolutely still except for the insects or birds that would pass through its cone of light. A common expression might give a sense of these little wells of darkness: a black hole. There were many of these black holes or, rather, the landscape itself was a vast, insatiable one. There, in the realm of the concealed, everything seemed lost and nameless. I've read many novels in which the dark is an inverted reflection of light. This was not the case here. If there is beauty in the world, Delia and I thought, if something moves us to the point we are unable to breathe; if something presses our recollections to the very limits of memory, so they can never be as they were, that something lives in darkness and only rarely makes itself known.

As I said, when Delia told a story she grew even more distant from her surroundings; she'd get so immersed in what she was saying that she couldn't be torn from her thoughts. Something might interrupt her, anything, but Delia would immediately pick up where she left off, more insistent and engrossed than before the distraction. This was not stubbornness, but rather a unique form of persistence; one more trait I have since been unable to find in anyone other than her. As soon as she left it in the hands of her friend, Delia forgot about the skirt. An article of clothing traveled from person to person, place to place, sometimes worn—in Delia's case, in the ideal way—other times inside packages or bags, wrapped in paper, folded or rolled up in purses or backpacks. An untethered object exposed to the elements that, contrary to what might be expected, was not reduced by its circulation, but rather acquired greater meaning and renown because of it. No one cared who owned the skirt; this followed from a certain truth, which is that no one did. Its mandate was simply that it be returned. This may seem emblematic or symbolic of something else and, basically, it is; but it's also true that this was how it happened in real life.

As we felt our way along in the dark of the neighborhood, we were covered by the starry night sky. The heavens were so flecked and the earth so black that it felt as though we were at the bottom of a cosmic well. I thought of Delia's friend within the simple walls of her home and convinced myself that, in her way, she was still guiding our steps. At one point, I remember, some drawings left scattered on the sheets had caught my eye. I leaned in to get a better look and Delia's friend made a gesture of irritation; she tried to hurry over to hide them from me, and was embarrassed to find that she was too late. I examined them. More than figures, the drawings represented movement; for example, the movement of a hand rubbing across paper on a dirt floor. I don't know why, after showing me so many things, the lady of the house would rather I didn't see these pictures. The first thing that struck me was that, if the marks depicted anything, it was largely the processes that produced them. Some of the images were faint, others less so, and their texture was varied or consistent depending on what they had been pressed against; others were delicate, a single upward stroke: perhaps someone had rejected the instrument—the ground in general—and held the paper up to the edge of a stone . . . I thought that the precise and extravagant surfaces were trying to say something, but that they were employing a language, a form, unknown to me. And because of this they remained mute, at first glance, like Delia's friend. I imagined the children and adults of the household occasionally spending time tracing its surfaces, choosing a patch of ground and making a print of the pressure they exerted on the earth. The paper, a few pages carelessly torn from a school notebook, would remain as records of a certain time, a relatively limited one, considering the duration of the world. But in their simplicity, which translated into a sort of eloquence, they seemed immortalized as the symbol or incantation of something that, though it hadn't happened yet, already manifested itself as evidence of what was to come. Perhaps I'll return to these tracings later on. Anyway, as I was saying, on those walks through the outlying neighborhoods I confirmed that nature holds greater sway in the dark, just as beauty does. If we employed all our senses, we could hear the crackle of ants marching across the ground, the same way the smell of food, though faint, indicated what was being cooked inside the invisible houses. I don't know. What I mean is that we were humbled by those nights: in the face of such immensity, anything we might do would simply be a consolation or an illusion.

I don't know. I'm standing in front of the mirror now, in silence. One can search for a sign, just as Delia's friend did for hours on end, then find it one afternoon and not understand how it could have remained hidden for so long. I remember the day I happened upon the low mirror. That's all this place needed to feel like a hotel, I had thought. That morning I had woken up with Delia on my mind, probably a thought that had been dragged over from sleep. I hadn't even opened my eyes yet and, as always, I was already entertaining some trivial idea. I thought: it must be morning for Delia, too. That was all, there wasn't much more to it. That sort of banality was enough to create the illusion of a routine. As I walked to the bathroom, I listed Delia's possible activities: waking up early, having a bite to eat, thinking about the factory and about the child, and so on. By then, I knew nothing of her life, and yet it was her, the memory of her, that rescued me every morning from complete indifference. That day, then, temporarily spared from the swirling waters into which I would sink when evening came, I went into the bathroom, stood before the mirror, and was surprised not to see my face. Reality had shifted, and no one had noticed. For a moment, an absurd idea came over me: I was afraid that the bathroom had moved. The mirror reflected a stomach, serious and expressionless. It was my bulbous abdomen, in appearance not unlike a barrel: swollen and stout, dense with skin and hair. And I had to acknowledge that, though startling, reality had been fair in its dealings, that the mirror's new position was not a threat, just a warning, obviously from the past. I thought, immediately, how thoughts of the future have been abandoned, how everything is a struggle over what has happened, or what no longer does. I thought of the child, who would one day contemplate his own round belly, a belly not unlike this one that had pressed against Delia's with the unexpected, though predictable, effect of conceiving him.

At times I've thought that if I'd heard about the child from Delia, I wouldn't have left her. Though this is no excuse, if there should be an excuse at all, the way we learn about something inspires our reaction, whatever the facts may be. I've read many novels in which this happens. When I found out about the child, I withdrew past the corner of Pedrera. It was a truth so unbelievable, so unjust. Finding out from someone else made me realize that I had abandoned Delia long ago, and that reality was simply reading my indifference, prior even to this outcome, assigning a greater significance to my actions than I believe they actually had. So I turned my back on the matter and dedicated myself to that train of thought, that "reading" of reality. Although my involvement had been decisive—I was, after all, the child's father—I felt removed from it in a way that would have been inconceivable a few days earlier. I felt the touch of an invisible hand on my skin, a hand from another planet that marked and condemned me. The first thing I thought was that I should apologize. If it was impossible to heal the wound, then I should at least do what was necessary to dispel it quickly in the day-to-day of these earthly confines. But, since I couldn't see the hand that touched me, there was no way for me to know of whom I should be asking forgiveness.

That hand, I thought, came from the future; it was the touch of the entire species. As such, there was no one in particular who could pardon me . . . Before that day, if anyone had told me that I was about to give her up, to abandon her, erase her from my world and cut off all contact, I would have been outraged and not believed a word of it. Delia was everything; she occupied every emotion and thought, at all hours, guiding every act and digression without meaning to. But the fact remains that I used the nine months the child needed to take shape, grow and emerge from the mother to distance myself, to avoid and pity her. This may seem contradictory, but that's how it was; pity and obliteration, or the other way around, if you prefer. Either way, it was what I imposed on myself. From that moment on, there would be two: Delia on one hand, and the mother on the other. The mother of the child, and Delia, the subject that preceded the mother. What began as a tremor within her, probably in the empty shack in the Barrens, had, ultimately, turned into a child.

By then the woman who would meet Delia on the corner of Los Huérfanos, a neighbor or a relative who lived with her, I think, had stopped going to wait for her; I did, instead. In winter, when it grew dark earlier, or when Delia had to work a late shift at the factory, a building a few yards from the corner would emit a steady white light, uncommon in those parts, which was made use of in the loading and unloading of cargo and the transportation of merchandise from one truck to several carts drawn by mules or horses, or from several carts to one truck. There were pushcarts with four wheels, which they called shuttles; these were used to move merchandise from one vehicle to another without having to lift it. This was the use made of light at Los Huérfanos: the moving of goods. One truck, two or three carts alongside it. The men moved in silence, their backs bent, while the animals waited, impassive. Strangely, the light didn't reach the opposite sidewalk (or what passed for a sidewalk), that is, where I would wait for Delia; this produced an effect that resembled stage lighting, as though the work were the focal point of some sort of performance. When she got off the bus, Delia would place her foot precisely at the edge of that light. Right then the shadow of the bus confused everything, making the night seem darker than it was, but as it faded into the distance Delia's feet would remain close to the border. I spoke before of her natural tendency to occupy frontiers, thresholds and transitional spaces; the placement of her foot was a rehearsal of this trait. Similarly, she'd occupy the periphery of the group when she went out to the yard with the other, stony-faced, workers. It was a physical periphery, because she ended up situating herself at the furthest edge of the group, barely a distant satellite, the presence of which is purely coincidental and which obeys forces beyond the immediate scope of the gathering, but it was also a symbolic periphery, the result of her being a woman, or a belated girl, among men hardened by physical labor. I remember how the deliberate bustle of unloading, the effort, the halting steps of those who moved between animal and truck, were to me a precursor of the leisurely pace we would soon settle into when Delia stepped off the bus. A few yards from Los Huérfanos began the black hole of the darkened street, confined to a realm of junk, the promise of houses and imagined cross-streets. The bus, which had just dropped Delia off and was still clearly audible despite its growing distance from us, was nearly the only trace that spoke, for lack of a better phrase, of a community. To be there was to witness the early attempts at a collective will, the rudiments of a coming-together that, through some strange paradox, contained within it the impossibility of its realization. Had they read these signs in time, the few settlers of the area would have known that they would never amount to anything as such, that is, as settlers.

Delia was tired when she got off the bus; the factory consumed the workers' strength slowly, patiently. The machine that she, in a sense, operated was hundreds of times her size. Beside it, she appeared still more vulnerable and slight. Off to one side there was some sort of workstation or counter, this was where Delia was supposed to work with several pieces at once while the machine ran smoothly, without her needing to attend to it. Given that it was doing Delia's work, it was logical to assume that the machine was a kind of substitute, but, on the contrary, the fact that she hung on its every noise, observed its operations, corrected any irregularities and adjusted its mechanical movements from time to time together made Delia feel as though she were the auxiliary component. This muddled sense of responsibility exhausted her: it was the machine that was in charge, that set the pace, so to speak. Standing before something so coarse and rudimentary, Delia also had to perform an archaic task: that of monitoring, though some of the processes and most of the details were beyond her. Given its tremendous dimensions, it seemed incongruous that a being as small as Delia could operate it. She was able to tell by the noises it gave off whether everything was running as it should; its clattering, like that of an old train, would mingle with its pneumatic convulsions; its uniform whirring, which sounded more like a whine or the whistled language of sea creatures, indicated that a fluid was circulating through the machine: not only that which powered it, but also another, some raw material. The machine consumed many things, aside from the workers' labor, Delia would say. Energy, raw materials, time, effort, and so on. As the machine performed its task, Delia would perform hers, which was twofold: to listen and observe,

and to sit at her workstation and put her hands to use while the for-
midable clanging of enormous hammers emanated from every corner
of the factory and mingled with the general din. Just below where
the factory ceiling met the wall, there was a window. Light filtered
through the entire factory from that single point, making visible the
particles that floated in the air. One night, a little while after getting off the bus, Delia told me that she couldn't remember how she
had started working there. This made sense, given that she considered anything related to the factory to be a virtue; it was a point of
pride and was doubtless what endowed her with her fullest and most
complete identity, the trait that allowed her to feel like herself when
confronted by the outside world, without shame. A feeling akin to
omnipotence, or something like it: the world could threaten to end,
to stop existing from one moment to the next, and the worker would
be the figure best suited to prevent its collapse.

I've read many novels in which people live in a world without time;
I mean, one without linear, psychological, or cosmological time, or
any other kind. Reduced to acting on a few instincts, an animal of
any species has a more tangible effect on time than man does. A
person closes a book and is surprised by the abyss of the day to day,
with the varying scales and speeds of time, fast or slow, which leave
a fine, invisible layer on the surface of things. Like dust in an empty
room, these layers settle uniformly and without hurry; the difference
is that they accumulate without building up, so they are always the
same thickness and can be lifted as one, regardless of how much time
has passed. Like time, which cannot be seen, these are invisible layers that cannot be touched. I'll give you an example. The character
in this book is an immigrant laborer who has reached his twilight

years. In his home country, he worked from the time he was a child, but a complex process of mental ellipsis has led him to believe that he only started doing so after he emigrated. The fact that, from the time he was eight, he left his soul on the bleached, unpredictable soil of his village from Monday to Sunday, is stored in his memory in a different form, not under the heading "work." He thinks, for example, of the wheelbarrows of shit he used to have to cart around, and what they evoke isn't the hardship—the missteps, the frustration, the cold, the dark—but rather the time that, suspended, refused to pass. It was a rickety old wheelbarrow, heavier than what it could carry, overflowing with whatever his family had unloaded into the latrine over the course of the year. He knew that his father's steps had left their mark on the path, prints too big for his own feet. Each time he stumbled, the experience confirmed that he was walking a course someone, none other than his father, had followed before, leading him to think that time advanced only through the repetition of actions. These were not the repeated actions of the deranged, the absentminded, or the desperate, but rather a repeated representation, the footstep that conceals the one before it and anticipates the one that follows. As though the subject were the action itself (carting shit, chopping wood, weeding the garden, and so on), and not the person who carried it out. This gave the boy the feeling of inhabiting a static, lasting, monotonous time. Nonetheless, he realized that this immobility was relative, because just a bit farther ahead he would use the last of his strength to tip out the contents of the wheelbarrow. This thought, simple and undeveloped from various perspectives, indicated to him that irreversibility permeated the base and the sublime in equal measure. It wasn't that he was especially moved by cyclical things—seasons, gradual variations in the landscape, work in the fields—it was that he felt himself part of a time that was free, compact, and tightly bound; impossible to break apart.

Now we return to the present. Many years after this "not working," as he sits in his pensioner's armchair he inadvertently overhears one of his sons allude to Einstein's train. He could understand the idea— the logic was fairly simple—and it seemed to be the best explanation for the anxiety he would feel when he thought the contents of the wheelbarrow might spill on him. At that moment he came to suspect that the fields, the house, his family, his chores, and even he himself were inside the rail car that the genius had used to explain his theory. The example had an immediate retroactive effect: entire blocks of memory were dislodged in the way that, when you forget one language, your former life is translated into a new tongue. Just as when he was a boy, he liked nothing more than to eavesdrop; not because he was drawn to the shameful or the improper, but because something within his bleak interior needed that complement to life found only in secrets. As he listened to his son, the man came to understand that it was not simply one of those ingenious paradoxes of the mundane; more than that, it was the explanation that allowed him to understand his origins and his new life, as he called it, in contrast the one he had led in the village where he was born. And so his memories, which could be transported back and forth from oblivion, did not belong entirely to him; they were part of the multi-purpose car that contained his family and the land. At some point he had gotten off the train, and since then had occupied his own, autonomous time. The multi-purpose car: it was an idea particularly well suited to what it was meant to communicate, a collective journey. The man was surprised to have reached old age and to have retained of his past only a simple token, devoid of value, and proof only of itself.

One question had always unsettled him: What could have made him casually blot out entire parts of his life? Now he understood that the mistake lay in trying to find causes or reasons. Trains serve many purposes; the answer could be found right there in the son's example. It was a simple comparison, an established metaphor—somewhat worn, but for this very reason, effective . . .

The problem was that, though the argument allowed him to understand and justify his new beginning, it also showed him that it was not new: the metaphor revealed his former life, erased until that moment. He sensed in his body, shall we say, the different accelerations that something as ethereal as time can produce. As he sat in his reduced state in the armchair that had over decades come to resemble the walls around it, listening to the uneven murmur of the voices of his sons, who were almost certainly unaware of him, the man revisited his afternoons as an accelerated stream, a continuum of eating and sleeping. The protagonist wondered about the meaning of these events, whether they might be a sign that the end was near. Each breath, every mouthful of air drawn deep, brought with it the scent of the dusk from his childhood. The same thing happened with sounds. He would have to take the wheelbarrow several times to the pit, which would later be covered over once and for all with dirt. This annual task, of resounding simplicity, seemed now to be the most decisive act of his life. One can imagine: rural time, a fixed cycle as precise as the solar year, as discrete as a whisper, and as encompassing as the world. But it wasn't only that. That sense of time had been broken when the child had left—or, rather, been torn away—and there was no way for it to keep moving forward. He was caught in his memory of the past; the story was compressed until it reached a speed at which it occupied a single moment, beginning and end, something living that resembled an intangible trace, as ethereal yet verifiable as a shadow. So if I were to say, "That man is me," my meaning would be clear: in life, one occupies different times.

Delia did not work for long after she got pregnant. The stony-faced workers, as I've described them before, would collect money in order to help the child along. A nebulous emotion filled the hearts of many of them, something between compassion and solidarity. On one hand, the group was making the necessary preparations so that its newest member—one of their own, most likely a future work-er—would face the fewest possible challenges. On the other, there were plenty of occasions to curse the world and pity the child who would be born into it so insignificant a thing, a solitary castaway. From one moment to the next, the orphan would enter into a reality that was not only hard or merciless but was, above all, incompre-hensible. Delia's fellow workers could not understand it. "Another one," they would say, "another mouth to feed." And, a few years later, there would be two more hands that would have to add them-selves to the collective labor. Thinking of it that way, as if it lasted only the flutter of an eyelid, time seemed to pass more slowly in the abstract than in practice. And yet it was shocking to see it all laid out in advance, as though life were just a day in the factory, waiting for the years to pass the way one waits between one blink of the eye and the next. Anyway, while the workers muttered about the child's arrival and secretly organized donations to help Delia out with a few things, I spent most of my time shut away in Pedrera. Like everything else around there, like everything everywhere, the buildings were laid out in a way that was not only imprecise and arbitrary, but also inconsistent and extremely dense. This became even more obvious when you had to cross through one house to get to another, when you wanted to leave Pedrera, or when you ended up in a space that, though it was private, belonged to several houses at once. For example, my bed was next to a hallway that joined two rooms to a bathroom, which, for its part, had to be passed through to reach a cluster of houses that had been built on the far side. Sometimes I'd think about the geography of the place and find no words for the binding and eccentric routes it imposed on those who lived there, as though the simple act of walking through it were a ritual of submission to its authority. From my bed, I would watch people pass with astronomical regularity, day after day, as persistent as ants. I thought: I, who have always so admired the working class, was heartlessly abandoning the weakest representative of the species as though I were intent on its extinction. It was an idea that did not lead to any other; it lingered only as long as it took to smoke a cigarette or hung there for a moment as the voices of passersby distracted me. It was an inert phrase that did not lend itself to replies or associations, nor did it translate into words, and even less so into actions.

The morning I heard, in passing, the words "There goes Delia, the girl from the factory that got knocked up," the certainty that something had changed shook me like a bolt of lightning. I was walking along Los Huérfanos; it was afternoon, and people were lingering in the vacillations of the siesta. At some point, from among a group of men leaning against a wall emerged the voice that said, "There goes Delia . . ." I looked up and down the street but didn't see her; not then, nor when I ran to the corner. I didn't know what to think, but I remember what I felt: instead of doubting the comment, I felt that not finding Delia right then confirmed it was true. She was hiding from me. The afternoon came to a stop; time was an ellipse in the middle of a void. It seemed as though the world were falling apart and that Delia had gone over to the side of evil. To this day I have no memory of the route I took on my way back. Who knows where I ended up wandering, I must have gotten lost looking for impossible shortcuts. If anyone had seen me arrive at Pedrera, they would have said that I wasn't so much walking as dragging myself along. Not long after, I would be subjected to another blow, which, by the cruel mechanisms of pain, modified the first: I found the neighborhood, and especially the area around my house, steeped in humiliating normalcy. There was no sign of my tragedy there—life was content to go on in its distracted way. It was at that moment, just as I was about to reach my front door, when I felt that hand from another planet touch my body. Delia belonged to the past. The vision I described earlier, the worker who watched years unfold in the blink of an eye, was the same vision that told me that Delia belonged to a past that was at once recent and unfathomable. I said just now that she had gone over to the side of evil. This belief has stayed with me, though now, due to the obvious workings of time and memory, that evil might seem less evil and more innocent. But, then again, there's something hidden behind all that, isn't there? Something that makes it ominous: Delia's innocence was a form of giving herself over to what might lie in store for her, including, obviously, my own actions. Because of this, the depth of her innocence made the evil that I inflicted upon her all the more definitive. These were the things that caused me the most grief. I wanted to sink into my sagging bed, wanted the furrow in my mattress to be a bottomless pit from which the smoke from my cigarettes spilled incessantly, like breath from the mouth of a volcano. And that's what it was to live: passing from one embittered trance to the next. My life scanned out to a meter of minor, insignificant actions. For example, every pack of tobacco was important, every cigarette unique; every movement of my hand was categorical, every exhalation of smoke definitive; every trip to the bathroom the last, and so on. I know the syntax of despair, not unlike that of disorientation. The world feeds on fantasies, bitter ones; people spend years believing in something, an illusion that comforts, rescues, or excites. As you can see, I was thinking like someone in a state of collapse.

There was something about Delia's situation that, though it did not contradict her becoming a mother, did contradict my unexpectedly becoming a father. It was the fact that she was a worker. This may seem outrageous, but it seemed to me that the world had thus inflicted another injury, in this case the second, upon her through me. That she, an innocent victim incapable of rebelling, had been conquered by evil despite her natural condition, which fell within the realm of good. There may be few things less worthy of mention than the injustices of the world; these are ideas that don't generally soften the heart. For this reason, I have not found a way to explain that things should have been different with Delia. The fact that she was a worker, as I said before, was not particularly objectionable to me; to me it was part of the order of things, an order that sometimes appeared cruel, as it did now, though there was always a certain wisdom to it. But when Delia became a mother, her condition as a worker would become secondary, the hidden backdrop of her persona. Her proletarian virtue would remain a virtue, but it would fall under the shadow of another, terminal condition. And I, who had always dreamed of passing through life without leaving any trace, saw in Delia's position as a factory worker a good match, precisely because it meant being with someone who lived on through objects but only on the provision of effacing herself, of slowly becoming nothing as her exhaustion and the part of herself that she gave over to her work increased and her energy waned; I, who had always trusted in these things, discovered, in a treacherous twist of fate, that it would not be so, that the child would live on. That was my side of it, which might seem a bit selfish. On her side, things were probably no better: we all know how it goes for mothers who work in factories, in a world made for doing one thing at a time and, in fact, for being only one thing in life.

One day, some time after returning the skirt, we walked for an entire afternoon without speaking. It goes without saying that walking was a dance imposed on us. It's the most lasting and accessible pastime, and the one that requires the least money. The desperate walk, but so do the free. Nor is it worth mentioning that, until night fell and the Barrens opened themselves up to us, we had nowhere to go. Delia and I looked like a couple of lunatics, walking from one place to another down paths that led nowhere in particular. Sometimes we'd see dead cats in the lots as we walked along side roads; the lighter ones could be made out from a distance, the effect of their bodies crushing the tall grass into the ground. This suggested that a force greater than their own—greater than their weight, in any event— had flung them down in the vegetation. I've read many novels in which death cannot impose itself over nature, despite its attempts. In these scenes, however, it had succeeded: the silent bodies of the animals that, through the detritus that surrounded them, announced that their last act had been that of being tossed. As for the rest of it, as our silence grew longer, the landscape showed us its unchanging face. Delia saw no mystery in the indistinguishable structures that, solitary, imposed themselves in the middle of the lots as a mass of bricks, iron, stone, and prefabricated parts within which a second nature, different from the natural one and unique to this kind of material, seemed to act.

We followed a fence that surrounded an endless field; off to one side there was a pond no more than nine feet across that had been given the exaggerated name of "the lake." I thought to myself that Delia's silences proceeded from her thoughts, and that those were of the factory. I thought that, just as Delia passed her energy into every object that moved through her hands, infusing each one with a bit of her own essence, so too did the factory, as a thought, claim a small but meaningful space in her memory, if only to remind her that it was an inalienable part of her identity. There are mental states more static than thinking or sleeping; in fact, they are even more passive than what is known as having one's mind "go blank." Such was the single notion that occupied Delia's thoughts as an idea of the factory. The alienation of manual labor has been widely discussed; its causes, forms, and consequences have been analyzed time and again. Still, alienation is not quite the word for the floating, yet sharp concentration that seemed to be meant as a defense against nothing in particular for Delia's passivity, with regard to her own mechanical movements. She transported herself with her mind, just as she seemed to be somewhere else now, as she walked beside me. And it was this gift, this ability to withdraw without absenting herself, to abandon me without leaving my side, that was most aligned with her nature. That evening, the fields that stretched out to our right and our left as we walked seemed like rustic parks with an unfinished plaza set haphazardly in the middle of each. Anyone could see in it the hand of man and notice straightaway how deficient the endeavor was in such an open, listless expanse; the hurried, half-finished labor that confronted the steady growth of the vegetation shrank before the renewed proliferation of the land. But the hands of that someone who wanted to plant a garden probably never existed; we had come up with the idea of a garden ourselves when we discovered these lots that seemed to have been built up and abandoned at the same moment, as if by someone not really there. And so, Delia's unique absence during that walk was like her torpor in the factory; they were variations on the same disposition, simply applied to different situations. To save myself the trouble of finding what might perhaps be more appropriate—but less expressive—words, I'll call this torpor or absence of Delia's her "proletarian disposition." The truth is that I don't know whether workers have a particular idiosyncrasy to them, though after meeting Delia and a few of her colleagues I tend to think that they do. In any event, I use the phrase as a simple association: the detachment in certain fundamental situations, like that of being at the machines, repeated itself in Delia in a number of different circumstances. A kind of absence, perhaps related to the quantitative actions that workers perform. Earlier I said that quantity, to a worker, is a quality stripped of calculation: the pieces can multiply infinitely, the operations divided into their most minimal expressions, yet they will always be the object of non-material thoughts—not of the factory's inventory or the company's gains, but of the abstract nature of accumulation, something akin to the science of numbers. Regardless of its scale, this numerical sequence projected its imprecise condition onto the objects themselves and, through them, directed itself first at the consciousness of the workers, and then to the world at large, the time of the everyday. In this way, Delia remained herself even though we were miles from the factory; an invisible thread connected one to the other. She turned her gaze to a copse of trees that, silent until that moment, suddenly came to life and stood out against the landscape; as the trees became more visible, it was Delia who began to disappear. The same thing happened with the stones and the animals we came across from time to time, and with other things, as well. She had a special capacity for imparting an overabundance of being; not a longer life, but rather a more emphatic presence. This quality, by a predictable mechanism of compensation, tended to distance her, dilute her, and make her nearly transparent, like I've said, just as happened every day when she took her place at the machines. In short, to continue with the comparison, this is precisely what workers do: they infuse the objects upon which they fix their attention with an excess. I don't know if these additions improve the objects in any way, nor does it really seem worth thinking about; in any event, as Delia proved, they do make things more apparent.

It is night. Until a few moments ago, I was sitting on the bed, looking at the floor and not thinking of anything in particular. I was beginning to sense that time of waiting that amasses in the middle of the night, formed of drowsiness and stifled sounds, when something like a sign brought me to my feet and over to the window. Once there, I saw the silence before I saw the dark: a false murmur floated across the air, a hollow reverberation that came from nowhere in particular, but rather from the night as black as pitch. It's true, what I said above, that nature rules the darkness; one felt that if anything came from this void, it was a combination of the varied and the indifferent. Those moments that are often called, in novels, "the pulse of the night." The world rests, the night churns; the day shudders, the world goes to work. For obvious reasons, the night is more profound and more cosmic than the day, but it's also the moment when the scent of the earth, from elemental waste to the scents brought out by the dew, prepares to reveal itself. And it's this combination of opposites—the breadth and impassivity of the celestial sphere, the galaxy following its distant course at full speed through the middle of the universe, and the singular labor of the earth, opening seeds and decomposing bodies, as persistent as an obsession—that is sometimes called the murmur, or the pulse, of the night. As such, I'm not sure I could say that anything in particular "called" to me. Somewhere in that night as solid as a trench carved out of darkness, I happened upon the light of a window suspended in the air. An old man was lying in bed. The lamp mounted on the wall lit one side of his body. Meanwhile, behind me was that other murmur, the hallway that absorbed the sound of bodies in their rooms at night. At one point, the man changed position, reclining a bit further. The wall in his room was an ashy color that may once have been white. It was striking to watch his minuscule movements, barely perceptible and yet somehow eloquent, like the way he would delicately lean one side of his body against the wall as though he relied on every particle of the building in order not to collapse entirely. My mind turned to the work of disease: a defenseless body in the middle of the night, waiting for the illness to cease or at least to rest, to be present for the story's final moment. For his part, outside that room but also in darkness, someone next door is thinking of the ailing man. On one hand, the depths of this illness, which expressed itself through the torment of the body, on the other, the night following its steady course in the middle of the vast expanse. I imagined that there was a message addressed to me in this convergence, and that I had only a limited time, the duration of the night, to interpret it. Meanwhile, a few faceless men hovered around the door, waiting for a sign to enter. They were standing vigil around the patient, or closing in on the condemned. Soon they would be doing the same with the deceased. I stared at his window; after a while it seemed that his body began to dwindle, its light fading from within, his skin grew duller still and his meager clothes lost their form, as though they lacked flesh to cover. I hadn't taken notice of the person himself and it was startling that now, in spite of the circumstances, I could see these details. It's probably because of the dark, I thought; the idea passed without leaving a trace. A path cut across his room, the marks of steps taken in life. A trail that indicated an old habit and a single destination, the diagonal line that stretched to the window from near the bed where the victim now lay. I was left thinking about that, and about the night, about the whim of the heavens and the resolve of that window, which combined to show more than was visible. The world could come tumbling down, I said to myself as I faced the darkness, and we would still be held up by the light coming from a room. My thoughts turned to animals: what does a beast feel when it encounters another life in the middle of the expanse? I don't mean the reflexes of a species, the operations that regulate action and passivity, but rather the moment of tension when the profound solitude of the animal gives way to the realization it is not alone. At that first moment, I said to myself as I stood at the window, the animal feels sustained by this other life, because it knows that the pulse that gives it strength is shared between them. The terminally ill man realizes the same thing, I continued, because anyone about to die recovers that original insight, his primal instinct. In any case, the night continued along its course layered with deep breaths, changes in temperature, and involuntary tremors, like when a nocturnal bird nearly flies into us and beats the air with its wings.

Writing about that night, as I am doing now, and remembering those spent around the Barrens are two steps of the same movement.

Before, I slid into the depths, unwarily following my course. Now I pause, frozen. It would be a mistake to call this a comparison, nor is it an association, but rather something more autonomous, a nucleus of memories made up of two parts, without either of which it is nothing. Something like the two faces of a medal or a coin. From then on, thinking about any aspect of what we call night—certainly as abstract as the day—has meant reclaiming a time in which my encounters with Delia unfolded according to a stealthy, clandestine, and anonymous order. We'd lose ourselves in those immense wastelands, visible only because we were together, walking side by side through inconceivably vast territories only to learn, with a mix of pleasure and surprise, that an invisible guide had led us back to our usual lot and the shack built on it with enough time to embrace and do something at once furtive and precise; on these occasions we would sense that, though it existed outside of time, the night had a measure, a magnitude that was patiently and laboriously abandoned in the attempt not to mark the hours. I don't know what effect this had on Delia, but it gave me pause; though I was pretty sure that I wasn't causing any harm, I was afraid that I was committing an ill-defined act, one somehow gratuitous and cunning, selfish and merciless. In the night, that mass of dark and unknown substances, as I said above, Delia offered herself up with the bewildered trust of an animal, so much so that it would be easy to think of her as a defenseless victim. Still, even if the opposite were true, it would be hard to say it was otherwise. Delia would clutch at me in a way that was agitated, urgent; a way that, by its very nature, couldn't last without exhausting its intensity. One could say it was love, or the anxiety produced by the night, I don't know, or that it was a burning, deep, and avid passion trying to break free, her way of submitting to the darkness and renouncing the factory, and so on. In the shack in the

Barrens, I was well aware of the moment when Delia stopped hearing the murmur of things, the drops of rain on the sheet metal roof, or the furtive scurrying of vermin. She was entirely open, turned inside out like a glove and detached from herself as she waited for something that might be fleeting or definitive, but was always overwhelming. In those moments, when Delia gave in to abandon with the urgent need to receive, I felt extraneous, as though I controlled nothing; it had been enough for me to take that first step, and now I was on the outside. From a certain perspective, my intervention might seem essential, but if it had any effect over Delia's actions, these excluded me, turning me into something at once transitory and abstract, though, as one might imagine, these were moments of tremendous physical agitation. It might sound exaggerated, but I felt further from her in those moments than I did when I would stand outside the factory and watch her during her break. In this way, Delia never ceased to be enigmatic to me, regardless of whether she really was, or ever wanted to be.

The animal feels sustained by the life of the other, I repeated, standing at the window. Night, I thought, the depths. I've read many novels in which the truth reveals itself during the night. But it is a conditional truth, because it relies on the threat of daybreak to show itself without reservation. At night we're the center of things, just as happens when we look into the past. I turned away from the window and sensed, as keen as a dagger, the pressure of a gaze on my back. Hidden out there, in the dark, someone was watching me. I wanted to know who, from where, and why. These were the questions of someone sustained by another life. I looked down, not knowing how to react. Animals do this, too, when they find themselves momentarily at a loss for a response. I saw marks on the floor that reminded me of those in the other room: I was another of those who etched little paths in the floor. As in nature, these tracks spoke of habits, repetition, and direction. The path, definite and well-worn, started at the door of my room, but split two steps later along predictable courses: the window, the bed, and the wardrobe. The path to the dresser was the first leg of the journey toward the window; the main one, as well, given that it was longer. For its part, the path toward the bed was a second detour, though it was actually more of an estuary: a broad and undefined, though discernible area which, though it did not lead anywhere in particular, spread like a stain made of light toward the wardrobe. Suddenly, the memory of that other room made me wonder whether this whole scene was not meant specifically for me. Something unusual had just happened, I thought; naturally, if I was the only one to notice it, it must have been directed at me.

This is the room I walk around every day. Before, Delia and I used to walk through the city and its surroundings; now I keep to these four walls. Sometimes the memory of Delia comes to me like something not of my waking mind. Not something from the world of dreams, about which we know little, but from that rarely accessed part of reality in which something is about to happen, but ultimately never does. There's no need to give examples of the supernatural, the magical, or the everyday; I know many novels that already concern themselves with that. I often think of Delia as someone, something, that pulled back just as it was about to take on another form, one thing on its way to being another. And so everything I've said, and memories in general, are more a mystery than they are a matter of nostalgia. Because I always end up with the same inconsequential, imprecise result: a memory that is more or less accurate—the events, the endless series of actions and circumstances—but is vague when it comes to the true meaning of things. There could be many reasons for this, though all begin, develop, and conclude with Delia. As I might explain later on, Delia generally appeared as an enigma. I have never seen anyone make their presence felt when so clearly trying to do the opposite, to disappear, splinter among the many objects that surround and threaten us. And Delia did this without trying. Silent, remote, and distracted, she always seemed one step behind the present. It came naturally to her: she was at once effective and incomprehensible, and, of course, invisible to the rest of the world. How could this be? Though I don't really have an explanation, I am going to attempt one: Delia was someone who pulled back. For her, time did not advance, and though it clearly didn't move backward, either, it occupied contiguous dimensions in which progress and retreat, or even slowness and speed, were eliminated as practical possibilities. This state of "pulling back" also meant that she always occupied an earlier moment, almost never the present. Contact was unattainable, as was gleaning a sense of this difference. It was a gift that allowed her to be absent, as I have described several times before, without being entirely gone. But, of course, this "earlier" moment was misleading, since she was obligated to participate in the same time as everyone else. And so, in order for this and its opposite to occur, Delia employed an impressive number of involuntary skills that, one way or another, always ended up suggesting absence and regression.

I can still see Delia coming toward me up the avenue in the strange light of the evening; she is walking along the curb as though she were balancing on it. There's the faint light of day, already retreating, and that of the streetlamps, which don't yet illuminate anything. In the useless glow of nightfall, things seem to appear and disappear from one moment to the next, almost certainly at the whim of the air, which grants things a bit more life—that is, it makes them more visible—every time the temperature changes or the wind shifts, until night falls in anticipation of the coming day. Anyway, I can still see Delia in this erratic half-light, which was able to reveal something in the distance and conceal something just a few feet away. I remember her coming up to me, but I don't see her approach. I'm waiting for the bus to arrive, not thinking of anything else. Sometimes I watch the workers loading and unloading, lifting the heavy crates and walking around the carts; my attention rests on the animals waiting, horses or mules, the empty thoughts that must occupy their minds while the men go about their work. I imagine the smell of the animals, which would, at another time of day, reach me easily. I think of these things, ideas without a larger purpose, as though my mind were playing a game of abstraction. Sometimes an animal flicks its tail in a way that is more, shall we say, instinctive than walking; I look at the lamp that lights the scene and imagine that at least one of them must find it dazzlingly bright. I think of these things over and over again, in a regular cycle, when all of a sudden, as though all my senses were heightened at once, I am startled by Delia's presence. She is two steps from me, cut out against the darkness, and she pauses before venturing an uncertain smile. I say to myself that it's not possible, I didn't see the bus. Men and beasts pause for a moment that could not be described as long or short. Confused and flattered by my consternation, Delia explains that she came from the factory on foot.

Stepping away from the window, I turned out the light and started writing in the dark. At first I leaned forward, out of habit, to see what I was doing. Predictably, I noticed that I saw less than if I looked straight ahead. Looking down, the shadow was darker;

looking straight ahead a weak reflection could offer at least the illusion of depth. Because depth is found not in darkness, but in contrast. And so, closing my eyes, then looking straight ahead so as not to see anything but vague outlines and shadows in motion, I started to write. Without the vigilance of my gaze, first my hand and then the letters, instrument and result, seemed more autonomous than usual. I would set down a phrase and immediately feel it break free, as happens with landscapes once we pass through them. This is why it occurred to me, while describing Delia's embrace, so urgent and yet so profoundly feeble, why it occurred to me that freedom is always linked to brevity. Duration prolongs, enslaves—itself, first and foremost. These phrases, written blindly, passed in a moment; because of this, their life was not only transient, but also hasty. The notebook, the smooth pages, my arm resting on the paper, weaving the dream of my hand. I had barely written anything when I heard another murmur at the window. It's me, I said to myself, I'm hearing things. I've read many novels in which the dark has its own consequences: a character sinks into bitterness and pessimism, or into his negative thoughts until he is gripped by despair and the most destructive kind of suffering. And yet in reality, or rather, in this sleepless state, this nocturnal energy is quickly snuffed out; the mystery that the night represents, which gives rise to a wide range of metaphysical implications and philosophical deliberations, does not last it's like a flame that ignites and consumes itself. As I thought this, there was a change in the density of the air: imperceptible though it was, the light that came in through the window showed itself in all its variations. And so it goes, I thought, breathing in the subtle variations. After writing for a while in the dark, I realized it had other effects. The phrases appeared and disappeared, as I said, like the landscape through which we advance; thanks to this cumulative, or anti-cumulative, movement forward, I encountered the nature of waiting where I least expected to find it, and in a different form. One is used to waiting for things: mealtimes, the following day, the next event—actually, not much more than that; in general, anticipation constitutes itself by situating an event on the horizon. Well, the waiting that night was pure, made of nothing and without promise of any kind. I remembered the cast of shadows surrounding the Barrens in a silence so dense with anticipation that it took on a single, shapeless form. Hidden in the half-light, Delia's body shrank further still until it reached an immaterial state, her slight form growing more tenuous as it was infected by the weightlessness of the dark. In my room, I thought: the shadows then, the shadows now. The ingredients that make up every life are repeated time and again, I said to myself, like right now: having met Delia, in a manner of speaking, thanks to the dark, years after abandoning her I was once again finding some part of that truth in different, though similar, shadows.

Delia said something like "I walked back from the factory." Only then did I realize that I'd been waiting longer than I should have, that the beasts and workers loading and unloading had distracted me. The light shone directly on the animals' bodies, while the men's shadows snaked around their feet. Scattered on the ground, discarded merchandise that would soon be forgotten completed the scene of measured, or at least engrossing, activity. A rudimentary task, I thought: lifting and moving, loading and unloading. Why are we so easily distracted by elementary things, like fire, for example? There I stood, with my head in the clouds, as they say, looking at the sidewalk across the way, when suddenly Delia appeared and—without even having entirely arrived, emerging from the evening like a shadow—transported me to a parallel dimension, a complement reality, before I'd had a chance to get over my surprise. "It's nothing, I came from the factory on foot," her smile repeated. I didn't manage to get a question out at the time, but it was all very unusual. She turned and circled around in front of me; without saying a word, she took my left arm, ready to start walking—or rather, in her case, to keep walking. Had I asked, Delia could have responded truthfully, but I didn't, and so to this day I have no idea what she was not telling me. A payday pushed back, a transportation strike, lost money; there were numerous possible explanations, many of them plausible. Sometimes one doesn't ask for fear of ruining things, other times reality seems to conform to one's expectations, and questions seem unnecessary. And sometimes, as I said before in different words, one doesn't ask the question in order to avoid the answer one already knows. At the time, I knew very little about Delia, yet it never occurred to me to ask her questions. Questions frightened her, and perhaps made her weakness more evident. There's no need to repeat that Delia expressed herself in long silences, or that, when she did speak, her words always seemed to be too few. Not so much because what she said was incomplete, but rather because you got the impression that during the brief time you had been hearing her voice, which was itself weak, something that had been on the verge of being said had taken on a different form, one that was just as communicative as words or gestures, but of another kind of eloquence. It was a negative eloquence, the realm of the anti-word, at the opposite end of the spectrum from silence. Her reserve was that of a worker, which makes sense. A muteness made of nothing, but categorical nonetheless. It is often thought that the most hermetic types live in rural areas: the shepherd who says no more than he must, the silent islander, the inscrutable farmer. People of an arboreal silence that is perceived as being profound. I think that the silence of people from the country is a reluctance to talk, a kind of ignorance or shyness; that of the worker, heir to the other side of muteness, however, is a complex silence run through with intrigue and contradictions, developments, distractions, and, above all, moral implications. The worker's silence—I know this because of Delia—is static; unlike rural silence, it transmits nothing, or very little, and when it does, its complexity makes it a contradictory form of communication. This lack of expressiveness becomes a stumbling block that disorients us, offering incongruent yet mutually reinforcing messages that can't be understood as a group, but don't exist separately, either.

I trusted that the meaning of those silences would come to me, to no avail. The scent of summer, which lingered into that autumn due to a persistent wind from warmer parts, brought with it the self-fulfilling promise of the seasons. The scent of water, of gradual decomposition, and of spontaneous rebirth. When Delia arrived and took me by the arm I understood, as soon as I heard her remark, the extent to which she occupied a different time, one that had not caught up to the present moment. This, as I said before, was one of the traits that made her unique. The subtle way she occupied a slight afterwards, to put it one way, or a slight before, a sort of chronological "barely." It was from this delay that she spoke; perhaps this is why her voice sounded so weak and why her words referred to something on the verge of being left behind, something that never took place at that precise moment. That was how she moved, along two different tracks. She would be with me, for example, she could have felt herself entirely at my side, and yet there would be a part of her that wasn't there. And when I say a part, I'm talking about time, not space. This, of course, might be hard to take literally, but I can't say it any other way. Before, I suggested that Delia had a number of simultaneous existences. One of these stood out: the one that was true, the product of her work in the factory. That building, which seemed so solid but was in fact old and in ruins, radiated one of the few forms of truth, that is, being the place where things were transformed, where human labor combined with inert materials to produce merchandise, those objects one later buys, if one can. That coarse yet important structure was also a ferment of emotions, almost always individual, which were experienced in that unique dose of existence characteristic of the worker, who was often unaware of them. This did not make them any less natural, though they could occasionally seem artificial. Some time later, the mystery of Delia's return from the factory on foot would be revealed. We were listening to the first stirrings of the birds as night came to an end; we had left the Barrens behind us and were walking along streets so dark it seemed as though, in that place, the night were nothing more than a vast and inevitable black hole—undivided, as Borges would say—when Delia began to explain to me, in her fine thread of a voice, why she had walked back from the factory that day. It turned out to be a long story. What started as just another comment made after a couple has walked a long time, sated by love and confused by weariness, became an actual story that Delia had to recount over the course of several encounters. A person, whom we'll call F, had been caught in the net of accumulated interest imposed by the moneylenders who surrounded the factory. Not all the workers had been able or willing to help, and what they had scraped together hadn't been enough to pay off the debt. F had felt it necessary to wear a disguise every day on his way in to the factory, and to leave wearing a different one: it was his only option. Sometimes the disguise was a stratagem, other times a theatrical ruse enacted against the backdrop of the wide gates of the factory in order to avoid being recognized by his creditors. He was in no position to head out to the yard during the break, either; F had to stay inside then, hidden, observing the movements of his fellow workers and the watchful eyes of the moneylenders, who would gather on the other side of the fence to wait for the day to end and, in the process, for him to appear.

Workers, Delia told me, are not always paid enough to cover the things they need. That's why there are people who make loans, because when Tuesday comes around and the worker has to make do until he is paid on Friday, often not even having enough to cover transportation, the extreme, and sometimes only, option is to turn to them. These are subsistence loans: they might amount to the value of a few round-trips or food to last a couple days. And because of this, because they aren't considered "meaningful investments," just as those who take them out aren't about to mount large-scale operations, they are charged the highest interest rates. Ten can turn into twenty over the course of five days, Delia told me. The smaller the loan, the higher the interest. There was a sort of penalty for taking out small loans; the moneylenders probably had no other way of guaranteeing their business, which was almost certainly limited. But then, there was also their tactic of harassing the indebted worker. Delia had to borrow once. It was a Thursday morning (the moneylenders go every morning except Fridays, payday, when they show up in the evening). She needed money to buy a bar of soap, which had run out earlier than planned. Faced with the alternative of not being able to bathe for a day, the household preferred that she take out a loan. Sometimes it's easier to go into debt that way than it is to ask something of someone who won't charge interest, Delia told me. It wasn't a matter of pride: if I understood correctly, it was an act imposed by collective thinking. Since money was a scarce good among the working class, it could not circulate in a non-utilitarian way, that is, in a way that did not satisfy a need. Goods that had no exchange value, like clothes, tools, or utensils, or even materials and labor, could change hands, but rarely food and never money. The proof that this was the effect of more than just the law of scarcity (that which is not abundant does not circulate) lay in the fact that the workers were ashamed to ask for money. Paradoxically, this led to their misreading the behavior of the moneylenders, whose onerous interest was viewed as a punishment, harsh but fair. Just like their proletarian identity, which is only acquired under certain circumstances, this concept of money belonged to the worker alone, contributing to the personal mythology of each and shaping the way their families thought about the world.

A disguise, a visual alibi. A word is not always just that one word, as many novels show. In his difficult situation, anything that could hide him took on the quality of a disguise for F, whether or not it had to do with his apparel. The moneylenders searched for him among the crowd, but eventually gave up thanks to the mimetic talents of the workers: dressed almost identically, their bodies had been worked over in similar ways by the similar movements they performed, and the way they all stood around, facing the street and the world beyond, these were things that effaced individual differences. As a group, they didn't look like anything in particular, though they were marked by their lack of differentiation. F's problems went on for a long time, but not long enough to serve as a lesson to his peers. Their exact duration was hard to discern, since they scanned out in trials and tribulations more than in events as such. At one point, the moneylenders threatened to stop making loans entirely if F did not pay off his debt, which had swelled over time. For his part, F never considered leaving the factory in an attempt to avoid payment; his alternatives were more radical. Taking his life, for example. The thing is, the worker is ashamed to be in debt, he feels it calls his very nature into question. In certain cases, like that of F, the inability to pay added a layer of tragedy because, deep down, he didn't see suicide as a last resort to avoid the problem, but rather as a payment in full. In a completely literal sense, he was capable of feeling that he should "pay with his life." The lender would probably not recoup his investment this way, but would be compensated by being proved right. And so, the meaning of money would once again be revealed through death. Extensive experience with loans, diverse and sometimes inconsistent feelings toward his debtors—a long history of managing such things had taught the moneylender to gauge the subtlest of reactions, and in this case he knew that F's evasiveness was not just a matter of not being able to pay, it was also due to his having discovered "the debtor's truth," as the lenders called it, which was that death was the ultimate guarantor. For their part, the other workers, aware of F's practical options and emotional dilemma, grew worried. The suicide of a worker meant the sacrifice of the archetypal member of the species, or the class, in this case. It's not that F stood out in any particular way; on the contrary, each individual needed to possess a degree of neutrality if he wanted to belong to the tribe, yet there are certain actions that plant themselves like flags, assuming a level of representation that had not existed before. It was precisely this circumstance, that the representation would inevitably be passive, as it was embodied by a dead colleague, that the factory workers feared.

As Delia recounted all this, I realized that I must have seemed like another moneylender when I would stand by the fence to watch her

74

during the break. As I wrote earlier, I noticed that I was surrounded by people whom I took to be curious onlookers. Perhaps the movements of the workers, that close, deliberate choreography that had seemed like some eccentric ritual, those steps that caught my attention for being so minute and insubstantial; perhaps those movements were part of the ruse, the disguise, meant to keep F hidden. The moneylenders stared intently at the group, just as I did when looking for Delia. And yet, as I recall, the gaze with which the workers met ours was somewhat ambiguous, at once an entreaty and a sign of indifference; there was no hint of defiance or indignation, nor, though this may be hard to understand, were they trying to deceive. It was the gaze of someone who just looked away but is still glancing sidelong to see whether or not they've remained the focus of attention. As is so often the case, it's at the point nearest innocence that the most vile or insidious scenes are produced, or at least the ones most difficult to assimilate or understand in the most general sense—that is, if they're not entirely incomprehensible. And so, the meaning of those moments escapes me now as it did then, though for other reasons. The scene witnessed from the other side of the fence, which to me was about the interest a few workers could spark during their break, as they dedicated themselves to the idleness permitted them by the factory rules, which were otherwise very strict, turned out to be scenes of surveillance and, in some ways, evasion. Delia already knew quite well that life isn't easy; young as she was, she also understood that things could always be worse. The only thing she hadn't yet discovered was that passivity can be limitless, and F showed her this. There was a strange approachability to the way F avoided his pursuers, which he did without really putting anything into it, as though it were a bleak and arbitrary procedure executed for reasons unknown. Proof of this was the listless or, rather, inexpressive demeanor with which he made only the slightest attempt to dissolve among so much matter. Few things generated a response in him; since every day he retreated a bit further into his withdrawal, this surprised no one. And so, F displayed certain qualities characteristic of the worker in a casual but pronounced way. Most notable among these was the pressure traditionally put on the worker to become one with his machine, not necessarily that he should join himself to it but rather, and more simply, that he should become its agent. I mentioned all this briefly with regard to Delia— her practical simplicity, her mental distance; in a way, these qualities found their fullest expression in F.

The menacing presence of the creditors had become inescapable: it could be sensed throughout the day and had a hypnotic effect on F, leaving him with just enough of a grip on reality to keep the production line running. According to Delia, several of the moneylenders were former factory workers. She said this in her half-whispered voice without any hint of emotion, but hearing it stopped me in my tracks; the solitary night emptied out even more. How was it possible that a worker, having fought so long and so hard to control his disdain for money, having spent so much of his life in a forced coexistence with its effects, how could that person end up reproducing it with such enthusiasm? Delia couldn't answer this question, nor was it likely that she'd understand it, so I didn't ask her. A former worker had a real advantage, she explained. He knew his ex-colleagues, and they knew him; even more importantly, he had experienced the religious fear that the working class had of money. By resisting, and in his talent for mimesis, F was a setback to the moneylenders, though in one of life's ironies he was unintentionally getting the best possible training for that far-off day when, as the saying goes, he would cross the fence. Many of the other workers worried about F, but most of them just seemed stunned. Seen from the outside, life in the factory might have appeared normal; only someone on the inside would have been able to sense the disturbance. And yet, the typical distinction between "inside" and "outside" was itself confusing and fairly useless, as was proven by the fact that I, on the outside, was totally unaware of what was going on, while the moneylenders standing next to me on the far side of the fence all those afternoons not only knew everything, but also played a central role in the situation.

In the end, a collection was organized; anonymously, so that no one would have to feel ashamed for contributing. As one might imagine, Delia handed over the money she had for the bus trip home; this was why she returned on foot. Her regret was immediate, a sense of remorse that lasted for weeks, as I clearly recall. Not for having helped F, but for having succumbed to the monetary order stamped onto all of history, and into that instance in particular. Delia remembered F's pained expression when a few of his colleagues gave him the money on behalf of everyone—though only a few had actually contributed, in this case the word "everyone" was not meant to extend the solidarity, but to dilute the dishonor. The debtor was shocked, his reaction half-concealed by a smile; though he was not aware of this, his trance needed to come to an end as quickly as possible. The delegation of workers formed a semicircle; F felt himself at the center of a false, poorly organized, and inappropriate procedure, a failed scene. He would rather have been dreaming and have woken to the menacing presence of an army of creditors. After the most extravagant and dramatic incidents, what remains with us of other people is always a face etched in the dark. Not in real darkness, but in the dark of evocation. Memories, strangely enough, have no light of their own. F's face, after weeks of pretending, received the unsettling news that it could—and should—stop doing so; this required a complex adjustment. It was impossible to know what was going through his mind. Though this could be said of anyone, it was confirmed in this case by observing the movements of F's face. A nervous smile searching for that unknown point where it could find balance, Delia told me; obviously neither relief nor joy, neither confidence nor vanity, radiated from it. The members of the delegation were not having any better a time. They stood motionless and silent around the debtor as though he were the center of an inconvenient cult imposed on them by circumstance. It would be easy to speak of donations, offerings, and so on. The workers adapting a domestic ritual enacted so many times in private, when they distributed what little money there was among the members of their family. These workers were absolving a guilt that could become intolerable at times, so they did something "bad," that in practice translated, as in this case, into something "good." And all of this was due to the fact that F, in a moment of insecurity some time in the past, had needed more to get by; one evening the money ran out and he needed to wait until the next morning to approach the lenders. In this simple paradox, I think, resides a large part of the silent wisdom that sustained Delia's fellow workers. In some way, this is what I meant when I wrote a few pages back that, in their way, workers suffer the world. I'm not talking about injustice in the abstract, which is always present, or about any concrete injustice, which can sometimes extend so far it becomes part of nature itself, but rather about a driving force: movable barriers that were sometimes invisible, and other times insuperable, stood between good and evil. The workers were

78

compelled to move between the two, unable to change them, but intuitively aware of their existence.

From the first time he sets foot in the factory, the worker is bound to a "good," but lives with the contradiction that practically everything he might do while away from his machine will fall under the category of "evils." Of course, the names of these categories did not come from the workers, having been classified and assigned by the time they appeared. At one point, the workers realized this and rebelled; the way they saw it, the fault lay with the machinery. So they decided to destroy those imposing, intricate masses of metal. They gathered the strength of their own weakness and struck out against them. That the machines buckled as though they were made of cardboard was no small surprise; at first, the workers were shocked—without realizing it, they had passed into a supernatural, magical world—the machines fell like a house of cards, and what just a moment earlier had represented the reign of force, a world that advanced according to the simple but efficient logic of the cog, now crumbled at the first blow; where they stood close together, they fell in succession, one after the other. Many of the workers were reminded of their own homes, their humble shacks, flattened by the wind on stormy days. But it seemed impossible that they should be witnessing something similar happen to the machinery. This could be interpreted as further proof of the frailty of the good and the indomitability of evil, but the workers perceived it in the opposite way: it was the instability of evil in the face of an immutable good. This relatively heroic legend was etched in the ageless memory of Delia's peers. And though many had no recollection of it or even any idea it existed, they were nonetheless under its influence—sometimes protective, sometimes innocuous or even destructive—and organized their work and way of life accordingly. Stories like F's arose, developed, and drew to a close against the backdrop of this legend. At first glance, the workers at their stations might appear to be practical and detached, but they were not pragmatic enough to be immune to contradictions or avoid second thoughts. Each payment received, every coin, represented to them the dominance of the machines. At the same time, they were not so naïve as to think that this perception was entirely real; they knew that their wages were only one part of the ultimate value of their work, and that they didn't come from the machines themselves. Nor were they unaware that the labor produced by their own strength was of little value in and of itself; that without all the rest, which was complementary but decisive, it ended up being insignificant and quite probably useless. To this natural complication were added other unknowns, familiar and widespread in their way. For example, there were those who worked without working. It's not that they were inactive, nor were they without responsibilities. They were simply people who did not consider what they did day after day to be work, despite the fact that it was similar to, or more difficult and complicated than, the work of others.

What Delia was trying to tell me was that the world of the factory was a special one. Irrational from one perspective, incomprehensible from another, and always that way. When things fell apart, as the saying goes, there would be nothing unusual about seeing the workers as a tribe of eccentric beings intent on getting through their shifts, keeping the drills calibrated and becoming one with raw materials and stages of production. But Delia saw in this routine, which had come to seem excessive, the bleak origin of the current state of confusion. She said this to me in different words, often in the form of silences and distracted phrases that in fact referred to other things, most of which were simple and even trivial, but which allowed me to imagine a substantive, though irrevocably hidden, order of thought. It goes without saying that these conclusions were always hypothetical, tenuous to the point of not having anything to do with Delia at all. I've read many novels in which characters draw arbitrary conclusions about other people. These ideas may be wrong, in fact, they almost always are, and so they generate all manner of irreparable misunderstandings, suspicions, and opinions. This, which is so common in novels, is even more so in real life. We live with our mistaken ideas about other people; life goes on as it always has until one morning, or any other hour of the day, some unexpected sign shakes us up, and we're left puzzled, aware that we had been in the grip of errors and falsehoods all along. At night, F was ashamed to go home. His family waited for him with their usual offhand acquiescence; a quiet shadow that disperses at the start of a new day and returns with the lull of the evening. F's shame had a single root, money, and two causes: having needed to borrow it and now needing to pay it back; like all good workers, he was horrified by the thought. All he wanted was to restore the peace that was living, doing his job, and, through a baffling economic operation that he found both strange and complicated, making enough to survive—to live badly, but to survive—as he often thought to himself at night, overcome by an absurd and redemptive hope for the coming day. Like their father, F's children were quiet people. Before he came home, they could be seen standing around in silence, as though in a trance. One might think that they were listening to sounds or words coming from within them, and that their skin, so delicate and pale it was translucent, was the outward sign of a desire to disappear, to dissolve into the landscape. Delia pointed them out to me once, a while after the episode of the loan, as we walked along a path we thought would cut through an endless field. We ran into F's boys where the path formed a corner with a dirt road that came to an end after a few purposeless twists and turns in a gully not much further along. It was strange, I thought, that the street should behave like a stream while the stream itself ran straight, the way streets usually do. Had she not known them, I imagine that Delia would have recognized F's children, anyway, because they carried themselves like their father; inscrutably, for lack of a better word. They stared down into the weeds, but didn't seem to be looking at anything in particular. It would have been easy to imagine those boys as future workers, I thought. The example set by their father, though somewhat hermetic, had certainly left its mark on the day to day of family life. Just as the farmer's body announces the work to which generations of his family have dedicated themselves, I sometimes thought I could detect, as I did in these boys, a "vocation" to the labor that they had been called upon to realize more fully in the future. One of them must have been about eight years old, the other not much more than ten. And even though I'd seen so much, when Delia told me that they had both been working in the factory for some time I felt, as one might imagine, a vague sense of surprise, a combination of disappointment and relief, of disenchantment and validation. She herself was practically the same age as the older of the two, though she had, until then, belonged to the world of adults, and not only because she was with me. With this revelation, F's children, too, stepped into our realm as the newest gods of the real, even as their bodies carried out childlike movements. Delia told me that the youngest workers were observed as they performed their tasks, that older ones were put to work at the machines, while the eldest were introduced to the world outside the factory—the moneylenders, for example. These stages made up the worker's education.

As Delia and I left the damp earth around the gully behind us, I wondered what F's children were looking for among the weeds. Maybe it was a screw, I said to myself, or a broken drill bit that was the reason for the search. Materials gone missing, a hammer without a grip hidden among the stalks. Boys: eight, ten years old. A span of time that might seem, were one to think about it, like the blink of an eye meant, in the case of F's children, two pulsing lives with a good deal of time behind them. As Delia and I walked along in silence, breathing in the listless summer air, in which humid scents mingled with the smell of plastic, I thought something like, "The girl that is Delia could give me a child." It was a spontaneous thought, as though something had just been shaken loose. It wasn't the desire to possess her, it was something more than that: the need to conquer, overwhelm, destroy, annihilate. I felt that Delia had something that belonged to me, and that if I didn't take it from her when I had the chance, I was never going to get it. The feeling was completely different from desire, and of course from passion, though I admit it contained a certain amount of the latter. It was seeing Delia as my enemy: only by at once destroying and worshiping her could I get what I needed, a sacrifice. The black hole that the fields became once the sun set—a barren stretch of land, a cave made of darkness that lasted until the next day—reproduced itself and followed its natural course—that of the night's advance and the astral movements one senses while looking at the stars—together with its counterpart, the pits of shadow along the ground that the light from the night sky doesn't reach; this black hole reproduced itself and followed the natural course of the night and all that it implies, on one hand, and on the other it showed itself to be mute, and most likely deaf, inside Delia. I'm not saying that figuratively. I mean "inside" Delia: literally, in her internal parts, her innards, as they say. The immense night, devouring light and time at a relentless pace, and Delia's belly, waiting to feed on my strength in order to dispossess me of something that did not yet exist.

The night was completely silent; the shadowy outline of the trees could be seen at a distance in the semidarkness of the starlit sky, like the contorted figures of an artificial landscape. I—or both of us, I think—felt we lived in a place that didn't really exist. A place you can walk through and find nothing but crumbling ruins and abandoned lots can't be called a city, but a territory so marked by improvisation and indolence couldn't be called the countryside. You could say a land like that, with its provisional nature and words that allude to nothing, would do no more than encourage depravity and animalistic behavior in its inhabitants. But we only felt the first impulse of this animalism, which in any event was fairly weak; an opposing force immediately restrained us, like a calm voice whispering into the ear of a raging man until he lowers his head in a gesture of resigned understanding. How was it possible to receive signs so contradictory that they would, under different circumstances, be mutually exclusive? I think it was because everything there combined to form a cluster of debris that was, ultimately, the remnants of nothing at all. One could trace the progression of one of these truncated signs: the fossilized flowerbeds, for example, in Delia's friend's "garden," which were really nothing more than little mounds barely raised above the forgotten terrain, marks left there as proof of a will to do something, but which now showed less the hand that had made them than the state in which they had been forgotten. This is what I meant by remnants of nothing, these superposed layers of inaction and neglect. The neglect was visible, though, masked as it was by the neutral workings of time, it could hardly be taken as a sign. And for one reason or another, the truth is that this stirred neither feelings, nor thoughts in me. This is what people really mean when they say "I didn't see anything" or "I wasn't thinking about anything." Incongruous complexities in which mutually exclusive cues meet emotions that are too vague, or too faint, to allow for any real judgment: this is when people opt for indecision.

F's boys were probably no more than a few hundred feet behind us; the question was whether they would still be staring fixedly into the weeds in spite of the dark, waiting for a mystery to be revealed there that almost certainly would not. There they were, dispossessed of everything and preparing themselves, in their way, for the bitterness of their adult lives, when that savage impulse I tried to explain earlier made me grab Delia by the shoulders and push her down with all my strength into the darkest part of the vegetation. I threw myself on top of her. Along with her lingering cry of surprise, as I hit the ground I felt an animal quickly scuttle off. I know what happened next, but am still ashamed to recall it. I can say that it seemed as though I were standing at the edge of an abyss, and that Delia was my only salvation. I would be lost in time, or rather, in oblivion; I'd vanish and, because all I had was the ephemeral imprint of a footstep or a glance to cling to, nothing solid would point back to me. It seemed this verification could only come from Delia, that is, from my actions toward her, which overpowered her will and, of course, her body. It was the child I was after: a wild animal howled, securing its bloodline. The feeling was completely different from the erotic attraction that joined us in the thistle barrens. I didn't care about loving her. I was driven by a more savage, more predatory impulse that I can explain, but find increasingly hard to understand. Delia came out of that scene in a terrible state. An innocent soul, or a wise one, she bore the shock and violence like one of those small animals that curls up in a ball when it realizes there is no escape. I remember wanting to go even further. I held her down, determined to cross through her, to feel her come apart in my hands. I wanted to split her in two, to feel her dissolve and slide through my fingers, but only so I could catch her, trap her, and subject her more forcefully still. Meanwhile the night went on, indifferent. Delia's terror had fallen silent, and in that silence the nameless flourish nature adopts in the dark could be heard. At one point I thought that the steady course of night was less human than it was irrational, that there was a good deal of madness, or rashness, or I don't know what, to the peace we call night, which was anything but peaceful. And it was that madness, which created the illusion of harmony in order to fight it, that had taken me over and confirmed, by some astronomical sense of justice, that what I was doing was, if not right, then at least fair. I thought of Delia as something incorporeal, a being whose mass of flesh vacillated between denying its depth and forgetting its material condition, and on whose breath floated something more than air: the encoded message by which she, as the ideal representative of her species, would perpetuate herself. I don't know why, but this quality of her breath was most fully realized when the denial of her body—in the sense of subjugation, conquest, domination—was at its most pronounced.

Delia lay there defenseless for a long time, as though unconscious. The moonlight made the scene more moving; I sat beside her body while she came to. She was not the victim of love, or passion; she looked more like the victim of a rape. I watched the insects that appeared out of nowhere settle on Delia's small buttocks, attracted by the glistening arches suddenly presented to them. Or maybe it was her body heat, I thought. I began to hear, once I had been freed of the crickets and the frogs, the monotonous trickle of the stream. Something began to flow again; the night settled in. Delia and her body. Subdued and so slight, it seemed impossible that moments earlier it had been the incarnation of a force that challenged me, an infinity that could not be contained or dominated. I thought: what's left of the city becomes more and more a part of the country at night, and not all the terrain that was lost is recovered the next morning. After what happened I felt sad and listless, and it occurred to me that this tableau, with Delia in it, epitomized the primitive charge of the scene. I felt a bitterness that was not unlike regret. I don't say this to excuse myself; it wasn't even a full sense of regret, but rather the selfish reflex of acknowledging, though it might sound pretentious, that after what had happened I was already condemned, that there was no turning back. Still, I thought, there in the night, one rarely experiences an emotion fully, these things are always approximations. Emotions can be sincere, but never exact. Delia's only reactions had been surprise, at first, then fear; later, pain and, at the end, shock. No signs of anger, nothing that would indicate resistance, or any sort of reproach afterward. I would have liked to know if this was an effect of her nature as a girl or as a woman. But they were both present in such equal measure, even mixed together, that I wondered whether the difference was, in a sense, illusory. On the other hand, since Delia was a factory worker, the difference was also irrelevant, as I've already explained several times; in fact, if the question continued to nag at me, it said more about me than it did about Delia. She was a nebulous being, to a great extent insubstantial, whose identity I needed to define.

The day came when I crawled out of my hole and back into the world. But "crawled out" implies a series of spatial maneuvers, and one might move around all the time and still be, in a figurative sense, in the same place. What I mean is that nothing had changed by the end of my seclusion; its only modest purpose had been to hide me, from myself most of all, though ultimately it only succeeded in making my ruin more complete. In any event, I had no idea what I was hoping to achieve. Apart from the reaction I described earlier—how, when I found out that Delia was expecting, I turned and ran like a man who had lost his mind, like someone who had experienced a terrible misfortune and was trying to protect himself without knowing how—beyond this reaction of walking blindly until I happened upon my own room, I didn't have the faintest idea of what I planned to do. This is what ruin is, this not knowing . . . It is a ruin I have never overcome. It doesn't matter whether my descent was fast or drawn out, unexpected or predictable, what made me miserable was how far I had fallen, that I had toppled from the heights of the most certain—though clearly not the longest lasting—happiness, to end up buried in my mattress. In the course of one short afternoon, I had descended to unspeakable depths. I've read novels that describe similar situations, which always seem trite, and probably are. Well, that's how I felt: I felt as though I were acting out the most pathetic scene in a story that relied on sentimentality to, as they say, breathe through its skin and unfold to the fullest. I thought, we are forged by the shapes of our emotions, even when these belong to someone else. I had made a child and then rejected its mother. That mother was a woman, a factory worker who had only just left her own childhood behind her, who had gotten me to adopt her world as my own without ever meaning to do so. And now I spent my days walking around my neighborhood, kicking stones, down streets and alleys along the sides of which windows opened onto people who had been lost in the furrow of their mattresses for all time. Windows covered by strips of fabric, pieces of cardboard, clothes hung out to dry. I knew very well how little darkness could be found in those houses, the static, buzzing heat of the afternoon that came in through the floor, the walls, and the ceiling, along with that resilient, intolerable light. The same thing happened with the cold. It was then, as I turned the page between paralysis and tedium, that I began to make out the voices of the children, a music that had always been available to me, but to which I had never really listened. In Pedrera, the cries, exclamations, and wails of the little ones spread according to their intensity.

When I left Pedrera, much of what had happened with Delia seemed impossible to me. Certain ideas stay with us all the time, like the combined proofs that tells us where we are and, oh, what we represent at any given moment. And yet, after my period of isolation there was no rule, no signs, that could help me understand what had happened. I mentioned before what goes on in someone's mind when they say "I didn't see anything," or "I wasn't thinking about anything," and so on. Well, something like that happened to me as I peered through the window, out of sight and not looking at anything in particular, checking the typical landscape of abrupt and asymmetrical elements, an ever changing, ever incomplete panorama; something like that happened to me as I leaned against the glass and repeated to myself, "I can't believe it." I, who had always felt such disdain for the tragic, even unconsciously, both as a way of connecting with it and a means of denying my own nature, which saw its own reflection there, now

89

had it right in front of me, with no alternatives or chance of escape. While I was confined to my bed, my tragedy had presented itself like the repeated actions of a bad dream. Episodes whose intensity had faded emerged from the monotony of half-sleep and, spent and discolored by repetition, called into question the truth of the very thing they were meant to convey. But when I left . . . It was another thing entirely to step out into the street, into the neighborhood, into the open. I felt as though the whole world were pointing at me. Not just as the man responsible for a cruel and depraved act, but as the person who found, in that act, the ultimate justification of his days. Neither forgiveness, nor censure, but something simpler: an identity. That was how Delia would become a part of my time, I realized that futile morning I stepped out into the street.

I've read more than one novel in which misfortune helps someone's bad luck along; I mean, there are people in these novels whose luck is worse than they deserve. This excess of adversity, like a surplus of evil, frees one's character of contradictions: the innocent become more innocent, the conniving more conniving; the lazy man is driven to the heights of laziness. Nuances and traits are, in the end, redundant: to give a simple example, it is of little use to the generous man to be uniquely benevolent if he ultimately turns out to be at the mercy of his luck. What I mean is, what happens in novels is deceptive. This story probably should have been much more awful than it seems, and is certainly much truer than it makes itself out to be, because the one thing I know is that, from the beginning, I felt myself involved in a tragedy without a statute of limitations. It is so easy to seek forgiveness, and so difficult to attain it, even when it is offered by the victim. For example, sometimes I wonder whether Delia ever forgave me; I immerse myself in the idea and go over the different forms of forgiveness, all of which are, in one way or another, misleading. There's something there that doesn't quite convince me, I think, these thoughts are a useless indulgence. Because Delia doesn't have anything to forgive me for. From one point of view, yes, but, I don't know, maybe she's better off because I abandoned her; at the same time, no, because my actions weren't directed at her or anything else in particular. This is why forgiveness is impossible, because it has nowhere and no one from which it can originate, or anything upon which it can sustain itself. An ideal system would be like that of the workers, I remember thinking to myself as I lay on my bed. When F had his problem, they started collecting money in silence, ashamed. And through this ritual of delegation, in the name of something abstract, like the threat posed to the class, or its pride, each made a contribution so that F could escape the threat of the moneylenders. A system like that would be ideal, because it absolved through the distribution of sacrifice, rather than guilt.

There was a practice among the workers, largely forgotten and rarely enacted, that was sometimes invoked in extreme cases, like that of F. An untold collective consciousness set off a mechanism lost in the reaches of memory, communal heritage, or the straightforward, but profound empirical memory of the workers. It consisted of leaving behind small sums of money, without any apparent reason or obvious logic, in places where the others would know to look for them in order to help a worker who had fallen into misfortune. These were not anonymous operations. Everyone had a role in them: the worker who cautiously approached to leave his contribution was the same person who would hurry back, strangely remorseful, to the normalcy of the corner where he worked. This made the ritual more effective, and more lasting. Because each lost himself, without compromising his identity, in the hope of a collective salvation, embodied in this case by F. Earlier, I mentioned the care he took with disguises once the moneylenders started trying to catch him. Now I think it's an exaggeration to call them disguises. Like Delia, F was always aware of his difference, even when it took the form of the smallest, simplest thing, the most elementary detail. This difference could serve, as it usually did, as a distinguishing mark, but it also inspired a deeper— and, as I said, simpler—feeling tied to the simplicity of the disguise. As workers, one of their deepest and most personal convictions was that of being different. The consequence of this was twofold: their identity set them apart all the time, and nearly any attire, in the broadest sense of the term, other than their factory uniform transfigured them momentarily. It was an inevitable disguise: a simple and natural costume, but impossible to change if the workers wanted to keep the face that was the source of their true nature hidden. It's hard to know when clothes become a complement of the truth; attire is an unnoticed trait that people adopt. And so the disguise came to permeate F's actions and his disposition beyond the appearance of the garments themselves.

I have little that belonged to Delia—mostly random, incidental things that on their own seem incomprehensible and useless: a dial, the clasp from a bra, a plastic lid. I also have a small button from her work uniform. I don't remember why she gave it to me; I suppose it probably wasn't on purpose. I do know that one morning, as I dug around looking for change, it turned up in the bottom of my pocket. I can hazard a guess or imagine something to take the place of this mystery. Something like a button, simple and superfluous in many circumstances, became, in the context of Delia's uniform, part of the factory's surveillance and control. One of the most humiliating tasks the workers were forced to perform centered on these minor objects. Since the factory sought an exemplary sort of discipline, it concentrated on accessory items and things of little significance. In this way, the company saw to it that nothing, no matter how small, escaped its control. It would have been easy to focus on the operators' attire, for example, through daily inspections of their uniforms, especially their work shirts, and so on. And yet the process was inappropriately complex for the circumstance, especially when it came to the inspection of the rubbings that the workers were supposed to have prepared in advance. They were rubbings that looked like the ones I had seen at Delia's friend's house. The only difference was that, instead of copying stones or the ground, these pictures were supposed to be of the design on their buttons. It was disconcerting to know that, once a week, an entire relatively qualified workforce was turned into a group dedicated to activities that seemed, at first glance, infantile. At home or on the corner, before they went into the factory, each one of them had to place a sheet of paper across the buttons of their uniform and run a pencil over it, then show the rubbing at the entrance. Obviously, each button was unique; if it wasn't, at least the workers believed it was. That's what had happened to Delia's button. It had probably fallen off during one of these weekly inspections and that night after work, as often happens between lovers, it had passed from her pocket to mine.

When Delia told me about those weekly inspections, I wondered if there was a certain group of beings whose mission it was to leave "rubbings," collections of marks akin to the things of the world itself. It would be a peculiar sort of "mission," given that its meaning would be unknown to those who carried it out; but perhaps for precisely this reason it would reach deeper, be more real, evidence of an original, powerful skill, an instinctive gift. At the end of the day, without these proofs and anonymous records—those made by anonymous beings, and those we all leave behind, which are anonymous in their own right—the world would be unbearable. I'm not saying that everyone should write or trace whatever they want—it's both good and logical that nearly everything is ultimately lost—or that the vast quantity of novels that exist should be some kind of substitute for Delia's friend's papers, or for the little round pictures the workers were expected to make of their buttons to show that all were where they belonged, that none were missing and that, ultimately, one presumes, no error or threat hovered over the factory. I'm not saying any of that. On the contrary, a while back it occurred to me that the marks anonymous people leave on the world, including those made on paper, are meant to oppose the written word; the novel, first and foremost. This conflict is not fought out in the open, it's not that one denies what the other asserts, rather, it is a secret and mutually unacknowledged fight. Among the infinite number of paths that exist, there are two that never meet. On one hand we have the world of marks per se—actions and events in general—and on the other we have the written word, epitomized by the novel. These two elements, like adversaries in perpetual battle, are precisely what lie hidden beneath the surface of fables. The marks of experience seek to eradicate, or at least diminish, the emphasis on the written word, which in turn tries to escape the redundancy of the marks (this is why it presents itself as a version). It is a fruitless contest about which we as individuals, as representatives of the species, have little to say beyond our anonymous contributions to the world of marks. It was likely that the pictures made by Delia's friend were also subject to some sort of periodic review. A game among family members, a community ritual, the proof of having been in one place and not another, a collective record ("the relics of the tribe," one might say), and so on; this is probably why she regretted my presence when I found them among the tangle of sheets: things like that weren't meant for the eyes of an outsider . . .

Meanwhile, the startled reaction of Delia's friend seemed, through a quick shift in perception, to be similar to, and almost connected with, the way Delia expressed surprise. It often happens that affinities make themselves known through similar gestures and inflections. It certainly seemed so that evening; in the way she fiercely defended her secret, which did not, or could not, rely on words, I recognized Delia's expression of surprise when she realized she had been found out, though I can't imagine two people who seem more different from one another. There's no need to explain that, just as Delia's friend seemed to be about to say something the whole time we were alone, her house, too, offered contradictory signs; these were sometimes obvious and occasionally vague or tenuous, even apparently irrelevant, which made the message they supposedly contained hard to decipher—if there was, actually, anything there to decipher. As corresponded to this art of selecting unexpected objects from the cumulative chaos around her, Delia's friend performed her magic trick with the skill of someone who had learned it amid adversity and neglect. The main purpose of this maneuver, which might also be assigned the term "custom"—being oriented, among other things, toward exhibition—must have been to repeat and perfect itself. It was a talent that suffused her other customs and actions, starting with the most immediate, then the loosely connected, and finally the furthest removed. An example of this was, I think, the hesitancy I described earlier: always being about to say something, but never saying a word. In this way and without realizing it, Delia's friend manifested the surprise she so masterfully performed when it came to presenting objects. Because showing something the way that she did, with mechanical precision but holding the gesture there for approval, or at least some kind of recognition, revealed the depths of her vacillation. I'll give an example. Earlier I mentioned the tin of combs, the roundabout way she had of showing me the pots, and her discreet annoyance when I found her tracings: I was violating the sincere—though limited—trust she had placed in me. I tried to connect her irritation with the meaning those pages held, or promised, but from then until the moment Delia returned, pushing the door open with her shoulder with the skirt tucked under her arm, nothing was the same. This phrase, which seems routine, is the essence of what happened. I've read many novels in which events bear no relation to what is described: novels that don't organize reality but, on the contrary, look to reality to organize their words. Nothing was the same with Delia's friend, though in what little remained of my visit nothing different, the same, or verifiable could have happened. Delia came back with the skirt, the friend stepped out to try it on and, as I said, we left right away. I didn't say anything then or later about the ideas I had at the time, but this clearly made a lasting impression. Around Delia's friend, her fellow workers, F's children when we saw them so engrossed, and everyone else associated with her—around practically everyone, at the end of the day—I always felt as though I occupied a place on the outside, that my role was to register things and draw conclusions from what I saw, whatever the circumstance. This quality was so strong in me that I gave the impression of being some kind of investigator, or very jealous. Still, though it was part of my own story, this world rejected me and so I observed it from a distance, feeling myself surrounded by and drawn toward a vague and impenetrable frontier: as I said a little while ago, a world that made up for its coarseness and extreme simplicity by the force of its eloquence.

Delia offered her world to me, while I, on the other hand, gave her little in return. But it would be a mistake to frame all this in terms of compensation, particularly with regard to Delia, who, as a worker, knew little of the typical utilitarian calculations that define most people's daily lives. As I've mentioned several times before, even something external to us like the landscape, in the most neutral sense, took on uncommon qualities when Delia and I passed through it, and this could only be attributed to her. The pockets of darkness were just as deep as always, but now they consisted of a reverse depth that neither folded in on itself, nor grew; I mean that they presented, let's say, a transparent darkness. There was a logic one always associated with the dark, a logic that proved, thanks to Delia, inappropriate and contrary to the true meaning of the word, which itself was also useless. Though she could not have known what she was doing, Delia showed me a new world, or rather, one that was renewed every night. This world, of course, had its own actors and its own rules. First, there were the factory workers, who yielded without resistance to the mechanical order of the line, and second, the factory protocols themselves, designed to optimize their productivity and make the most of their physical demeanor, which meant it was necessary to regulate both. Delia had the mysterious quality of concealing and revealing the things that, as they say, made up her world, without any apparent reason and according to a logic that at first glance seemed incidental. Actually, calling it "her world" is sort of redundant: it was a whole that formed part of Delia; she was made up of each element, no matter how distant, small, or superfluous. I don't know if this was due to some other logic of the proletariat, but

I do know that I felt more and more that reality, in all its manifestations and circumstances, reached me having passed first through Delia as though through a sieve; everything brought her to mind, mostly because in Delia I had found a way to see everything anew. This had its consequences: if, on the one hand, the feeling was becoming more and more constant, it also multiplied the signs of a repetitive world stripped bare that highlighted Delia's absence, that is, her negative proliferation. And so, on that afternoon as we walked away from her friend's house, I got the strange feeling that I was leaving part of Delia behind. We followed a trail that tried to pass as a road, and were soon outside the lot that belonged to Delia's friend. I remember an air of stillness, something like anticipation or a predisposition to inactivity; in other words, the light grew thicker, night fell, and the earth began to breathe.

There are dogs that will carry their quarry around for days. Though long dead, the prey seems to retain something vital for the hunter—if it didn't, it would have been forgotten, as happens when there is nothing left of the victim but a sad tatter of hide. Sometimes I imagine a brief dialogue, a diminutive fable without lasting significance: the prey says, "Please, no," and the hunter responds, "Yes" and carries out his plan. I don't know where these sudden thoughts come from, though the situations to which they seem to allude are often fairly obvious. In the universal language of entreaty, "Please, no" is a last request, already denied, made when the end is near. In the real world, this "Please, no" is almost certainly the most-repeated final plea in history. I think the reason the hunter does not abandon his prey, even when it's no more than a strip of leather, is that in it the scene of the "Please, no" lives on. On the vast plains, the steepest precipices, the solitary steppe, it's always the same. As Delia and I walked along, I suddenly wondered who was leading whom. Some part of what she offered meant everything to me; this is sometimes summed up by the word "love," though it's also true that a word can mean many things at once, and that these meanings are usually different and contradictory. At the same time, as I said above, I never knew exactly what it was that I gave to her. It can also happen that the hunter needs to drag the remains of the victim around because it is the only thing that allows him to forget the nature that surrounds him, the blind and bestial world he cannot escape. With its compulsory passivity, the former prey condenses the details of the scene, bringing together all the qualities of their surroundings; the lifeless victim is thus the hunter's talisman, an anti-heroic "trophy." This interpretation may seem somewhat mystical, but I haven't found one that describes the situation better. Because that's what this is about, isn't it? Shedding light, sitting down to find an explanation that gives the question meaning. The definitive thing about magic is not that it proves the implausible can occur, and therefore that it exists, but that it attempts to show that the implausible relies on magic to announce that it is improbable. But sometimes the unforeseen does take us by surprise, not so much because it is unexpected, but because it is irrational. I've read many novels that try to present the supernatural as natural. A reality that had been concealed until that moment, lying in wait, reveals itself; nature is concerned only with hiding itself while characters submit to, are torn apart by, and retreat from its unfamiliar laws, and so on. The problem is that nature never alludes to itself, and the supernatural is the most innocent way it makes its presence felt. As we know, the prey gives life to the hunter.

Earlier, I mentioned the meaning loans tended to have for Delia. The ownership of a thing was a secondary quality, one that might have a negative or restrictive effect, though this could easily be resolved by lending it out. Within the community of workers, or the social order of the neighborhood, objects sometimes attained collective ownership. The "owner" of something became its guardian, to put it one way, and everyone knew that they could use it whenever they needed, if not immediately, then at least without complications. This was expressed in everyday life, in even the most minor details and mundane circumstances. And so, eventually owning everything, or the greatest possible number of things, continued to be a dream for many or most of the workers, who knew very well how society in general functioned, but for whom all that had long ago turned into a mirage they recognized as useless. I think that, by lending these objects out, the workers were able to increase their density; to the material existence and primary function these things had, say, "at first glance," was added an unexpected relevance that was multiplied through their circulation and exchange: the objects became more useful the more often they changed hands. And this turned out to benefit the workers, whose own existence was lean and whose belongings, as we know, were few. Just as the prey gives life to the hunter, loans enhance the identity of objects. A hammer, for example, becomes more of a hammer the more often it is lent out. But the hunter gives nothing back; at least, not to the prey. If he does give something back, he does so in such an ambiguous way that only an arduous process of investigation and verification could confirm it. One of the most significant differences is that the hunter believes he is taking what belongs to him; he feels something like entitlement, which helps him spot, give chase, corner, and so on, and finally kill. Another fable, slightly longer than the last, might clarify this difference. In the community of workers, for example, "Please" sets their exchanges in motion; the prey says, "Please, no," while the hunter, as always, resorts to the habitual language of his monosyllabic "Yes."

I should say that I knew Delia would lend me life as soon as I laid eyes on her. I write this in a figurative, rather than a literal, sense. I was able to confirm this premonition; it is a fact that stays with me to this day, so long after the last time I saw her. I'm not referring to the enhancements that come with the circulation I just described, but rather to something more, a supplementary vitality, a fantasy made real that, in its realization, sets itself outside of time and above all other things, beyond what we take in with our eyes. I'll give an example. Right now I'm holding my pencil over my notebook, under the light, and the shadow—a slim pointer—crosses the blank lines of the yellow paper. Just like this shadow, with the depth and nuance it adds while reducing the color where it falls, Delia exerted a similar influence, faint yet absolute, over me. It doesn't matter whether she was aware of this or not—perhaps if she'd known, she might not have done it. In any event, though it may sound vague, I'll say it just the same: Delia cast a benevolent shadow over me. Like the tip of the pencil on the page, which not only writes but also projects a restless shadow that leaves no trace, or at least no visible one, I believe there were things Delia did that were meant to last, "to leave a mark" on me, and others that went unnoticed at the time and reappeared later, or were forgotten, and so on. In the first place, as is always the case, there were the memories, which require no proof. I won't say anything about their quality; there are few things less exact. On the other hand, to talk about all this would be to talk about the form it took, and all I would be able to salvage of that would be my own vacillation. At times like this, one tries to find those essential elements; obeying the law of memory, one focuses on the detail in an attempt to read the marrow hidden at its core, within its nucleus of wisdom. But only conventional elements can be salvaged this way, primarily physical details recovered in the form of faces, figures, limbs, and so on. What I mean is that, in order to salvage the past, to salvage that which is hidden behind things, we also need the concrete and mechanical objects and situations that give us life to this day; it is this past that sustains us, but it abandons us if we recover it exactly as it was. There is a lesson in this, to which we should submit ourselves with humility and patience. And all the more so in Delia's case, who, as I've said, folded in on herself even as she made her presence felt. A weakness that was part of her constitution made her tremble like the leaves. Upon finding herself exposed, generally after reacting to something, Delia would close herself off inside a delicate silence tinged with anticipation, like the moment before a glass breaks or the hunter attacks. These things were more than just bodies and faces, though they were, of course, expressed through them, making them conventional supplements. Something similar happened when her friend found herself exposed, both when I found her rubbings and when the man on the train handed her the distorted portrait. A reaction that lasts the briefest of moments, and for this reason might seem inappropriate or the result of some kind of disruption, but which leaves an enduring mark.

One day we saw F's children in an empty lot scattered with debris. Then, too, they were lost in contemplation. A few silent bags of trash had caught the brothers' attention. They stood there, motionless, looking down; after a while, one would lift his head and stare out toward the horizon, then immediately back at the pile in search of answers. Delia told me that looking at garbage was often a way of exercising the imagination, "What they don't have," she added. I didn't respond. My whole life, I had watched the same ceremony, and may even have practiced it myself, but it was only through one of those strange mechanisms of memory or conscience that, as I observed F's boys in action, their staring organized into periods of rest and concentration, I was able to recognize it as an act whose unusual meaning, if it could still be said to have one, was rich with local custom. The pastime consisted of unraveling the past: imagining the source of the trash—which was varied, that is, in the different substances themselves—and what had been done with it before it had been discarded. It was something that was done every day, an unexceptional exercise to which only F's boys, and only on that morning, could have drawn my attention. There were those who thought the garbage spoke, that it revealed a hidden truth through messages organized like that, like trash, the sole purpose of which was to be deciphered. And included in this "sole purpose" was the specific language required to read and observe them, which was activated by the analysis itself. The trash could be rural, domestic, or industrial. This collective exercise might have been an extension of the ancient tradition of reading the future in a system of signs, but which at some point had been inverted, and from that moment on was used to unravel the past. Was this further proof that the future no longer mattered? Perhaps the locals were rebelling against the linear, "historical" time that had so punished them, choosing instead the alternatives they had at hand. And so waste, material that had reached the end of its usefulness in the minds of many, had a bit of life breathed back into it: future or past, better or worse, it didn't matter; what mattered was that it was different. It's easy to imagine the limited repertoire of trash in a community so marked by privation, yet that was precisely why this was a favorite pastime:

because the likelihood of finding something unexpected, a surprise, was minimal. People feel a need to study the signs left by others; in this space of scarcity, there were plenty such traces to be found in the trash. They stopped to contemplate and compare. One thing with another, what was seen yesterday with what was there today, and these with something discovered a month earlier; an illusion of continuity maintained by the population because it lightened the load of the day-to-day. But it was evident that, like all others, this custom contained within it the seed of delirium. And it would probably take very little to bring it out: the slightest deviation in the routine, an unexpected combination, anything. Because the seed is a mechanism that waits for the right moment. So, for example, the whole of reality could be seen as a universe of garbage cast adrift, or like a choice or object that has been "wasted" relative to everything else, to what might have been, and so on. The traces, or rather, the marks of waste. Because ultimately this is an ancient endeavor, isn't it? There has always been something to decipher, a message waiting to be released.

In the thistle barrens, after we made love, Delia would sleep for three minutes, or maybe five. She closed her eyes, her body, and her mind, fully letting go of herself only once all activity had ceased. Afterward, she woke just like she did every morning, opening her eyes suddenly, before she was awake. Her eyes got ahead of themselves somehow; they were what woke her, not her mind. Once she was awake, we feigned a few playful movements as though we were going to start up all over again, but then immediately stood and left the Barrens, sometimes to continue on a walk that would last almost until dawn, sometimes to go back to her house and say our goodbyes a few feet from the door, where the latent presence of the others made itself felt, though it did not seem to be affected by ours. There were dogs around that could have been from anywhere, and a few lights shone so faintly that they seemed forgotten even to themselves, on the verge of going out as they cast their glow over an endless space impossible to illuminate. Delia's house, like everything about her, felt unique to me. As it had been from the moment it first sheltered the person who was, to me, a marvel of tenderness and beauty, who enhanced everything she touched, every space she inhabited. The signs of deprivation, how hard it was to carry on, and so forth, were visible in the house; these marks were indications of its admirable characteristics of autonomy and constancy, not of its abandonment. What I mean is that, if there were something exemplary to all this, the poverty of Delia's house was exemplary in the way it was indifferent to itself: a veneer made of silence and determination, exposed to the greatest neglect.

A light in the distance, a flickering streetlamp, marked the highest point in Delia's neighborhood, an elevation that suggested something historical, yet forgotten, both topographical—obviously—and undefined; more than anything, though, it gave the neighborhood a concrete identity, just like the corner of Pedrera did, where I lived. I've often thought these neighborhoods could never be the substance of a novel; even if someone were to join them together, one by one, like dominoes, or the way they appear on maps, until they became a single, vast amalgam of neighborhoods, even then, they would still lack the density required to be represented, if not to positive effect, then at least with some degree of conviction. On my earliest visits, it seemed that the wasteland in which Delia lived underscored her unique qualities. Like those deities who reign in solitude, her sublime beauty grew amid the greatest neglect. Sometimes her house seemed like a shack, other times like a collection of materials and random artifacts, arbitrary and unnatural at first glance, but consolidated through use and the passage of time. This continued use turned these objects into different ones: time dignified things that at first, I think, could have seemed incongruous, happenstance, or even unnatural. From this fact, as one might imagine, other lessons could be drawn. I am not going to summarize the materials and objects that made up Delia's house; I will not, for example, say cardboard, zinc, PVC, or sheets of plastic. Today, in the cold, I saw a dwelling the size of a person: two cardboard boxes bound together that, of course, ended up resembling a coffin. The cardboard was paper-thin, but in that moment was as resilient as stone. This was also true of Delia's house, the materials of which drew their strength from the need and the steadfastness of its residents. The past of these objects was forgotten forever, predictably, only to be recovered when they were no longer part of the house. But it was an illusory sort of forgetting, because it was only from this past that they derived their value as part of a dwelling.

From then on, it was not uncommon to see groups of people or solitary observers transfixed by garbage being stirred by the wind. One day a photo was taken in the street, or something like a street. It was a sunny afternoon; Delia must have been enjoying one of the rare days off that the factory gave her. We had been walking for a while; I was looking at the ground, the worn dirt path made of pebbles and little chunks of other objects, broken down by time and use; I saw these things and thought that the ground was as it should be, certainly as it had been for a long time and would be for a long time to come, but that Delia's presence added something special to it, a secret message shaped and revealed by her alone, which ennobled it. As I stared at the ground and kicked stones, sometimes without meaning to, she explained the rules of an unusual game they played at the factory: what it was called, how it consisted of dividing time into the smallest units possible. Since the appeal of this game was grounded in division rather than variation, the intervals got shorter and shorter, and were eventually impossible to verify. When they got to that point, the players started over. But the participants gained a skill through playing: they must have sensed it in the way the units got smaller and smaller, and so something originally begun as a means of killing time, in all the diverse implications this might have for a worker, became a reflex, a sixth sense set in motion on its own when the group's desire to play was stirred, usually by chance. It seemed to me that Delia took part in these games as a worker, like everyone else, but also as a girl: as a worker she needed to have control over time, to subjugate and incorporate it within her own nature so that, once hers, she could transfer it to the factory, which in turn converted it to a completed task. As a girl she was after something similar: to lay out the different dimensions of time so that, later on, she could reject them as untenable. In this way, the game found in her a dual, and complete, form.

Anyway, as we walked Delia explained the rules, the surprise and anticipation, the spontaneous synchronization, how the game was won, or rather, the fact that it was abandoned before a winner was declared, and so on; as Delia described all this to me, her friend emerged from the bushes—a few squat, dense tufts that formed an island that seemed darker than its surroundings—walking toward us as though she were stepping onstage. We stopped; she approached without ever taking her eyes off Delia. "Hi," "How are you," "Fine," they said. I remember she was wearing the shirt with fruits on it, and that she fiddled with the fabric in a moment of vacillation, just as she had before. Delia's friend had a camera with her that she was about to return; she wanted to take the opportunity to photograph us. Delia resisted, but without any real conviction. The photo should be pasted here, on the page, as proof of that afternoon. Delia's friend got us into position, moving our bodies with her frail arms as though she wanted to mold us into a different form; later, as she held the camera ready to take her shot, she found time to gesture to us with the other hand while asking us, quietly, to face forward and look at her. Delia and I stood side by side, with our arms around one another, wanting the camera to register that singular truth about to be set free, if only for a moment. I remember how Delia's smile was shy and anxious, and that her skin, as opaque as wood, was glossy in advance of the print. We didn't know it at the time the photo was taken. Only later, when we actually saw it, did we notice the people standing around a pile of something behind us. We had looked around for a while to find the best angle, and had found an ideal one: a gentle slope that suggested silence and neglect, a panorama that was ideal in its meager, but essential, symbolism. The silhouette of a factory could be seen in the background, a detail that couldn't have been absent, as present as it was in Delia's life. And halfway between there and the foreground, one could see the land descend along a slope that grew steeper and ended in a space the camera would never capture, a sad little dried-up lake. Posed there in our loving embrace, happy, enthusiastic, content, and so on, Delia and I looked at the camera as though "forward" were another way of saying "toward the future." Delia's friend lifted her arm, wanting to say something without saying anything. It was a blotch crossing the sky. I remember that the sun was in front of us, and that we had to squint while we waited for her to take the picture. The friend said something I didn't hear, of course, but this time it was because the sun blocked out the sound. An instant later, at a moment Delia and I didn't know to expect but which we recognized all the same, the afternoon stopped and we heard the camera take its shot.

I just mentioned a metaphorical "facing forward." Well, as it happened, the real "forward" had a "back" to it, invisible at the time. A back that didn't cancel out the ahead, that is, us, but rather turned it into a degraded image. Weeks, or probably months, later, when looking back on that afternoon would have required an unhurried act of memory, Delia's friend appeared with the photo. We were walking along when someone called out to us from maybe a hundred feet away; it was her, coming toward us with her hesitant gait, which at first glance simply appeared to be slow, but which was actually all weakness and exhaustion. As we waited, we watched her approach. The only thing she was carrying was the photograph. The way Delia's friend walked reminded me of her house, and I realized that movements as small as hers unfolded best in confined spaces, that they were more in their element on that scale. When she finally reached us, she held the photo out to Delia. For a while, we didn't know what had happened. Delia was silent, unable to express herself in words. The thing was, as far as the photo was concerned, we didn't exist. The sun that, as I said, had blinded us also kept us from appearing in the image. Our bodies were overexposed and only the contours of our faces, or even less, could be seen; our features had been rubbed out by the light. I thought of those paintings in which the artist conceals the face of his subject with a crude, thick brushstroke, a hurried swipe that speaks of a kind of silence, or at least of omission, haste, or the impotence of the image itself; that was what Delia and I looked like. In contrast, the group behind us stood out like a bird silhouetted against the sky. It was easy for them to rise to the occasion; meaning that each one of them showed the best of themselves, or at least the most eloquent part, as they stared at a pile of garbage in a way that resembled a rite performed before an altar or a fire. And there in the foreground were Delia and I with our featureless faces, marked by a stigma yet far removed from any ceremony.

I said before that this development surprised me; I should also say that, later, it seemed predictable. By triggering a secret mechanism, Delia and I made it possible for the group to appear. The photo had to choose and it chose them, salvaging the more primitive scene. The remote, the archaic, often imposes itself of its own accord. But it's also true that, of the two "scenes," both presented serious difficulties. There was the group of six or seven figures contemplating something, absorbed: garbage, in this case. This is what makes it "primitive"—this withdrawn stance seems less mundane than the one adopted by Delia and I as we tried to find the best pose or angle with our minds on the future, or our own photographic vanity. But it's also true that, from a different perspective, our attitude was spontaneous, simpler and, because of this, more ancient or primitive: we wanted to endure. The six or seven of them had been there for a while; the earth showed their footprints and where they had come from, each one different from the next. Their faces could not be made out, but they were all looking intently down and, though this can't be proven, were clearly deaf to the noise around them. The generality, among other things, to which all waste aspires is overturned by its contemplation: the garbage did not inspire indifference, but rather fascination, conveying its significance to those who observed it. In this way, the group was superior to us in more than just their number. It's very likely that more than one of them thought, before lowering their eyes again, that a father was being photographed with his daughter—a natural distortion upon seeing us together—and then went back to their series of associations. This is why people had such contradictory reactions to us when presented with the truth. Later, I might describe these expressions as surprise or confusion. For now I'll simply say that these reactions reached us—Delia and me, but especially me—as a reminder of what we were and what we were not, of what we could be and what we were allowed to be. It turns out that love is a great equalizer. Like our faces in the photo her friend took of us, the differences between Delia and I were blurred. But many saw our equality, something so obvious to the two of us, as impossible. Things that are but do not seem to be, or the opposite: the darkness that seems to be light, the favorable sign taken as a disaster, and so on; all this has been the subject of many novels. At first glance, things appear obvious, natural; they always seem to be something they are not, not just different, base, or irrelevant.

Now I look at the crust of hair standing at the mirror, the bulbous stomach working its way downward in search of more body, more space; I see all this and it's hard for me to believe that I'm the same person who, for example, took that picture with Delia. As I realized too late, some did not see Delia and I as being alike; we could seem to be many things, but never two people who were, shall we say, equals. On the contrary, the differences were often more obvious. As I said before, there are novels in which people face adversity according to the strength of their convictions and the measure of their passion, in which reality reveals itself through risk: the world is a formless precipice; unquantifiable, transcendent and, as though that weren't enough, one that seems to obey a central command. It goes without saying that this was not the case with me, and not only because I've distanced myself from the reality of novels. Delia and I felt united, made equal in our distinct but equivalent natures, by a general sense of indifference. The group reacted like stones or plants; nothing drew their attention from the unfocused contemplation into which they sank for hours at a time, just as nothing could compare to the distraction, that is, the neglect, transmitted by their actions in general. Nonetheless, it was true that we were subject to a form of surveillance that was at once vigilant, patient, and offhand.

Delia and I relied on the indifference of others in order to blur the line between us and, at the same time, to make ourselves disappear; as such, we looked at the outside world in the same way. There was an ideal we never put into words, though we always thought about it, according to which we had to let ourselves dissolve, eliminate what was unique to each of us and become something else, something unintelligible to others, but clear to us. Delia, the factory worker; me, the anonymous man. As a couple, we should have been transparent, embedded in the invisible backdrop of the landscape. But, as I wrote above, what one doesn't want to know is often exactly what is. The things we fear and willfully ignore, what we turn our backs on because we'd rather not know, the infinite facts we avoid and want to do away with, choosing ignorance instead; what ends up happening is that all this comes back to surprise us in the moment of our greatest solitude. Well, in the end, Delia and I were surprised to find ourselves marked, accused by all of being different, or maybe just unusual, but definitely not a part of the lethargy and indecision around us. I don't mean to say that we were special; on the contrary, our inertia was absolute, lassitude had taken us over. The endless walks we took were one proof of this: imperturbable and immune to exhaustion, we expended no effort. Nature, deceptive, had enlisted us to its cause, turning us into misleading creatures. For example, I'd look at the mud on rainy days and the first thing that would come to mind, after Delia, of course, would be whether that essential—in the way all mud is—mixture might not originally have been destined to form the foundations of another world, other people, or to mold a different nature. I'm not talking about primordial conditions, which have never interested me much; what I mean is that I wondered whether the mud might not have been called upon to hold up neighborhoods, events, a series of things completely different from those that had taken shape in reality; and whether, in that case, it might not have better fulfilled its role.

Mute as it is, one can't expect eloquence of mud. It expresses itself through quantity: colossal masses of material, or earth, which give form to the planet, the mountains, producing landslides, accumulations of sediment, and so on. But my question was directed at the unit, at the fistful of mud. I asked that absurd and arbitrary part of the whole—for example; what is left behind by a pair of shoes and later hardens—what those traces really mean. Of course, it was a question I never formulated, and to which I didn't expect an answer. It was the rhetoric of reflection; I asked about Delia, that other part of the whole, the same way. Accustomed to industrial controls, complex processes, and large quantities, Delia was unmoved by nature's extravagance. A passivity that could also be understood as a profound affinity, a level of acquiescence or solidarity aspired to only by those who are marked or chosen—not chosen by anyone or anything in particular, but rather are endowed with a unique sensitivity to their surroundings. In Delia's case, I believe this was intimately tied to her work in the factory: through mechanisms that were in one sense abstract, and in another sense not unlike the processes of production to which her own hands lent continuity, Delia made herself a protagonist of the perennially incomplete and apparently delicate machine of industry. This intimacy had the paradoxical effect of distancing her more and more from the things that occupied her thoughts and movements and, over time, resulted in a kind of ironic distance regarding anything that might be considered staggering or weighty, as nature often presented itself to be. It's true that I mentioned similar traits before, loosely calling them Delia's "proletarian disposition." But when faced with the natural landscape, the vast expanses of countryside, topography, or changes in the weather, this sensibility was not expressed solely as withdrawal or detachment, as was the case with all other things, but rather, as I just said, as deaf indifference, as an abandonment . . .

There was a certain irony to Delia. Looking out over the landscape, as that more or less harmonic arrangement of natural contrasts is called, a knowing smile would creep across her face, as though no truth found there could be new to her. A barely perceptible, though eloquent, expression that combined affinity and indifference, withdrawal and understanding. I'm under the impression that it was precisely her daily exposure to production and raw materials on a large scale in the factory that turned her into a being that saw magnitude as a cause not for admiration, but for acquiescence. Of course, this was a trait that she shared with the other workers. Neither landscapes, nor natural scenes had an effect on her, her internal fibers did not stir at any of it, natural or artificial. On the contrary, the humming of the machines: that was their lingua franca, and they turned to it in order to decipher the outside world. This might seem superficial, and also arbitrary, but in any event it was part of what, as I have said, made the workers the guarantors or supports of the world. Just as they did with their heroic legend, they returned to this language when they least expected it, even when they thought they were speaking another. It just so happens that workers, like almost everyone else, have been shaped by ideas and actions that are, in a way, external to them. I say "in a way" because no one, of course, could deny the interiority of their thoughts or the practical trance under which they acted; nonetheless, external things manifest themselves through people's ideas and actions. It's never the other way around: people do not express themselves outward; it is instead the outside world that manifests itself through individuals. I'll give an example: one of Delia's fellow workers. By chance, the two of them always ended up on the same shift. Another detail, far from insignificant, is that they were the same age; seeing them together brought to mind a brother and sister carried by destiny toward the machines. This person, G, did not stand out at all from the rest of the workforce. An invisible cable connected them all, through which a certain pace and level of exertion was transmitted; though it wasn't always the same rhythm, it was always shared. Despite the fact that he was still practically a boy, G worked with remarkable focus, similar to the concentration that took Delia miles from the factory, though even in those moments no world or sounds existed to her but those produced by her own labor.

G could sometimes be seen crossing the yard in a threadbare coverall with shiny buttons while the other workers formed groups over by the giant metal crate. Delia would already have climbed onto it and balanced at its highest point. He looked so adrift at those moments, an unformed consciousness taking the effects of its contact with the machines, under whose alienating influence he had been for hours on end, out for a walk in the scant nature of the yard. A few crumbs from his meager breakfast remained in his breast pocket; at his tender age, G had gotten in the habit of searching them out with his fingers and lifting them unconsciously to his mouth, lost in his thoughts. When the whistle sounded the end of the break, G was the first to go back inside the factory. He had to let his eyes adjust to the shadows; this took him only a few moments, and then he regained the determined gait with which he always approached the machine. The empty workstations looked like a life without life to him, and he was sad that he had left during the break. Like many others, it was only through participating in and leaving his mark on production at the machine that he found a tenuous, but profound, justification for his existence. G was in no position to recall his first day of work at the factory, but he sensed that life had not been real until that moment; he remembered it as a waiting period, an antechamber. Life before the factory was a fiction, not because it really was, but because that was the way he remembered it. Now, on the other hand, he was in the domain of reality. G obviously didn't expect it to end; fiction has a finale, reality does not. But these categories were about to change places, all that remained was for the drama to unfold. It happened suddenly one day, when he arrived at his workstation to find two machines; not the one he was used to, but two others. The marks of the old one were etched into the floor: deep, permanent traces that suggested the passage of time and a weight that was no longer there. At first, he thought the new machines would have the same functions as the other, and that he'd be able to work with them in the same way. But when he realized this was not the case, quite the opposite, that he couldn't have imagined anything further from the old equipment, he refused to work. The factory faltered in its daily operations; the vibrations of the machines, the robotic clatter of the assembly line, and the tireless whirring of the conveyor belts could all be heard as a symbol of the ceaseless labor of industry, but G remained immobile, transfixed by the old marks. It goes without saying that they fired him without the slightest hesitation; according to the factory, an "example" needed to be made for the other operators. A machine taken out of circulation created an obstacle: an obsolete worker. In this case it was G, from many perspectives the best in the factory: young, healthy, and disciplined.

But his reaction, though it originated inside him, took its shape from the outside: it was the old machine saying no that spoke through G, and to do so it chose the silence, or rather the stillness, of the boy. This was how the outside world, in this case the machine, expressed itself. G remained motionless in front of the marks on the floor and, though it had only been a few days, the memory of the old device came to him as the image of a distant labor: a singular, vague idea disfigured by time and enhanced by its simplicity. In that earlier time, harmony was, shall we say, an expression of brutality. It's hard to stop the labor of the workers when they are inspired, because each one senses the work of the others; it's a collective feeling that renews their drive and redoubles their efforts. He didn't know why, but in his reverie G remembered an old math problem from the factory: if a worker needed two days to make, for example, a hammer, how many hammers could ten workers make in four days? The workers would laugh at the way the question was phrased, in large part because of the emphasis it put on the number. The answer might be a quantity, in fact it might be much higher than what mere arithmetic might indicate, but what mattered to them was the advancement of the action, that is, the measure of activity combined with the passing of the day. Above, I suggested that the worker can't measure his own work; here I should add that this is because his work, and especially the product, the result, seems abstract, somewhat irrational to him, due to the repetitive nature of his labor; yet for this reason, it is also tangible, even weighty. The worker, a consummate expert in material transformation, is baffled by any attempt to translate the value of his work into an order external to the factory, like money or time. Their salary meant a lot to the workers because it was what allowed them to survive; at the same time it represented little, because they didn't know what effect their physical effort had on what they received or, for that matter, on what they were producing. This impossible translation was the source of the power that emanated from the factory and extended not only to the workers, but also to the true outside world, that is, the nearby streets and the community in general, reaching even those who were unaware of the existence of Delia's factory, in particular.

Stripped of the instrument that supplied his identity, G was forgotten by the other workers long before he physically left the factory. On that fateful morning, his presence took on an additional quality: that of a stigma. While his thoughts, as he stared at the marks left by the machine, seemed lost in that outdated labor, the other workers fixed their gaze on his expression, captivated by the threat it represented. In G they saw a likely future and a sorrowful past; though they may not have wished it, and though it wasn't entirely true, that was where they all came from; G represented some part of what they were trying to escape, to erase from their minds with one quick stroke. But they understood that the boy's troubles were not connected to linear time, that neither he, nor his "problem" represented a retreat or an advance, and so his refusal—and his very presence—were rendered abstract. G's was the worst kind of threat, because it took root so near at hand. More than a possible future or a forgettable past, which could have been tolerated with a bit of resolve, G was the tragic scene that held the proletarian life of the community together. From one day to the next, the boy had become the inverse of the factory as a whole, and his mind could not take it; in the same way, the workers found that part of their immediate world had turned itself inside out like a glove, bringing into view that which the choreography of the factory, the activity of the machines, the skilled movements of their hands, and the contortions of their bodies had always tried to keep from sight. As Delia would explain, one morning G did not show up at his former machine, or rather, at the new ones that were unable to hide the marks of the old. Though he had always been the first to arrive, during the crisis he showed up even earlier, only to leave long before his shift was over. It was strange to see how life outside the factory went on as usual while this tragedy unfolded inside. I say strange in order to be able to say something; in fact, it was devastating. The truth is that everything was the same inside the factory, too, aside from the moral threat posed by G and suffered by his fellow workers. But if many of the causes and effects of this anomaly were unknown on the inside, where it was produced, they were monumentally ignored on the outside. And this sparked a certain bitterness, because the world went on turning, unaware of G's terrible experience—either its beginning or its end. How many anonymous victims like him does the world produce every day? This is the true factory of man, though saying it in these words might seem inappropriate.

Delia and G. I've often thought that the connection between them— that concrete and enduring bond so pronounced that at first glance

119

they seemed to be brother and sister—remained vital despite G's dismissal and the different paths their lives took. The boy ended up being abandoned by the factory just like Delia was abandoned by me. The factory dismissed him for the distress he showed when faced with the new machines, filling him with even more suspicion and mistrust; in that same way, I turned my back on Delia and left her in the most painful state of abandonment. I recently mentioned the interior of the factory and the outside world, how one was unaware of what was going on in the other; now I want to describe how something similar occurred between the world in general and Delia's interior. However barbaric and cruel, my abandoning Delia did not disrupt the course of the world, which went on in spite of her suffering. The world also turned its back on something else that Delia and I knew: the cell of life that had recently settled inside her. This is how both of them ended up as victims, though of different things and under different circumstances. I remember Delia's expression: she couldn't believe it. To put it simply, she took it like a swift and fatal blow. Her eyes revealed her shock, opening wide with fearful uncertainty; she couldn't react, which was a form of reaction in and of itself. I also remember what she said, which was, as always, appropriate. "Don't leave me," she whispered. Now, writing these words, I remember the other two I wrote above, also in reference to Delia: the victim's "Please, no." I am unable now, as I was then, to make it better. It was not only Delia's eyes, but also her voice that had changed. It seemed to come from somewhere behind her throat, and sounded as though it belonged to someone else, a cracked and pitiful murmur. And I remember that, in spite of this, she struggled to preserve its inflection: it was she who spoke, though she seemed to be on the verge of becoming someone else. She took my hand.

"Don't leave me," she repeated. Perhaps, without realizing it, she meant to underscore her feelings, which were already eloquent in themselves. Like G, Delia reacted spontaneously. This was surely due to their youth; they were both practically children. The problem with reactions is that they are never clear in the real world: contrary to what happens in novels, where the most unexpected or complex action provokes, in the other characters, a reading or reaction that corresponds to its supposed obscurity. That's not what happened in my case. Delia and I once went for a walk. I've already said that there were uninhabited and diffuse territories that nonetheless had some form of community life. Then there was the opposite case, hybrid spaces that were less a neighborhood than an area that seemed to be made up of one multi-family dwelling: the streets were hallways that could only be traveled on foot, the plazas were no larger than patios. Similarly, there were also shared dining areas, often exposed to the elements, and a few sheet metal doors distributed around the perimeter of the neighborhood were the only way in. As was the case in Pedrera, once inside, things turned out not to be as they appeared from the outside . . .

Delia and I were walking around the perimeter of one of these neighborhoods or slums when along one corridor, or street, rather, we saw countless marks, people's footprints in the dust. One is used to coming across different kinds of tracks, so one could also get used to seeing, as in this case, many footprints. But there was something puzzling about this image of multitude that gave us pause; so many people walking, who knows where. We pondered this for a long time, surrounded by a silence barely broken by the sounds typical of the place. The street sloped unevenly toward us. When we realized

where the mystery lay, what surprised us most was that it was something so obvious, and yet so strange: all the footprints went in the
same direction. This might have been nothing more than a curios-
ity had we not found, a little farther along, a similar street with
footprints headed in the opposite direction. Walking around that
place meant passing through its houses or, as I said before, crossing through a single house divided into multiple versions of itself.
The walls had, at some point, all had their corresponding windows;
they—the walls—were made from a wide variety of materials. Just
then we ran into several old men who seemed to be headed to wherever they gathered every day. People walked in groups there, but
always in silence, at the most muttering something in that language
shared by families or tribes, a language made of exclamations, usually unconscious and unintelligible to outsiders, sometimes deaf as
well as mute. We saw a dog asleep in the shadow of an old sign. It
was still a long time before nightfall, so Delia and I ended up walking around the ample perimeter of the neighborhood before turning
onto a road that would take us to the Barrens. I remember that,
a little while after leaving the neighborhood behind us, we turned
and looked back. A disorderly cluster of houses could just barely be
seen above a dense crop of bushes growing in a hollow almost at the
horizon. The setting sun illuminated each differently, according to
the materials that had been used to build it. In this way, each seemed
to obey its own measure of time. Some were still in daylight, while
others were already in darkness; they belonged to an immediate
future, a recent past, or to ancient history. Later that day, after we
left the Barrens and the deserted shack where we would hide, we
walked a bit farther until we were a few yards from Delia's house;
there the silence was deepened by sporadic barking, and the darkness

seemed to tremble, its rhythm marked by the pulse of the surrounding countryside.

Footsteps, tracks, paths. Delia and I tirelessly recombined these words; walking was, for me, an obvious and practical extension of her company. Because of this, when I'd walk without her I felt I was doing something else, distancing myself from what I was born to do. It was the absence of something that belonged to and defined me, the feeling that something was missing and that I, also, was less. While Delia was at the factory, I was present in the world, or rather, I "witnessed" everyday life, observed people's habits, like talking in the morning, checking the time, and so on, and it seemed incredible to me that everything should appear to go on as usual when that which ultimately held up the world, Delia, was far from there. Actually, I could understand this behavior in people who were able to go about their normal activities because they knew nothing of Delia; what was beyond me was my own passivity in the face of such appalling ignorance. It might seem paradoxical, but Delia's absence kept me from taking action, from taking part in anything other than my habitual, useless, and ultimately dispassionate meditations. Delia influenced me despite the distance that separated us, much as she did at her workstation: thoughtful, absent, introspective, isolated, this is how I often imagined she controlled the factory. The way she acted gave the impression that she organized and directed every detail of the collective labor. Perhaps this was the only impression that could be drawn from work like that, which brought the rhythms of machines and of people together in a way that was at once harmonious and rushed. In any event, Delia, with her restraint and her focus, overshadowed and almost hidden behind her workstation, seemed to be the neural center of the community. Her influence, that force that emanated outward from Delia, its epicenter, extended first throughout the factory, as I said, organizing its rhythms and production; it also passed through the walls and expanded beyond them, insinuating itself into people's lives without their ever knowing it. Meanwhile, Delia went on as usual with her half words. Her language had an eloquent sparseness to it. I would listen to her speak, and think that her intermittent and, for all intents and purposes, inaudible, way of expressing herself confirmed her deep proletarian identity; on the other hand, she seemed like one of those characters in a novel who, with their one expression and few words—words that are often said by others, and are rarely their own—are able to move between books and endure in someone's memory. There was a law she obeyed: that of intermittent speech. But "law" does not entirely convey it, primarily because it was not in response to any mandate.

That afternoon, as we circled the camp after discovering the alleys with the footprints headed in the same direction, Delia told me that she thought she'd seen G, the worker who had been fired for rejecting his new machine. She had only seen him for a few moments, but it had been enough for her to recognize the terrible effect his dismissal had on him. Delia was making one of her habitual journeys for a piece of clothing, either to pick something up or to return it, an expedition that could last half a day or certainly several hours, taking unreliable transportation or, most of the time, walking. She was distracted, thinking of the appealing secret of clothing: the fact, paradoxical from many points of view, that getting dressed meant putting on a disguise, expressing something profound, or at least something that wasn't on the surface, through the illusion of hiding oneself; Delia was distracted, thinking of these things, when she saw

G standing motionless on some corner or another, not waiting for anything in particular, his hands hanging at his sides like weights. A few seconds were enough. She saw his childlike face hardened, overcome by dejection; he was probably miles away from where he stood at that moment. It was enough to show her how the lack of specific knowledge or a special skill, could, for a worker, be a deficit that translated into an advantage. Another worker who didn't know how to work the old machine and had never become one with it wouldn't have had any trouble adapting to the new one. In this way, G's aptitude became an obstacle. It's a hardship for a worker to know something, Delia told me, you can't imagine how much more useful they are, the less they know. The work isn't always coarse and brutish, but a lack of skill is often required to carry out their partial, or truncated, tasks, which have no justification outside the context of the production line. G was a perfect example of this. His wanderings through the lots around the city, which Delia imagined to have no particular purpose, were an attempt to return to an original lack of skill. The slightest ability beyond what was absolutely necessary was enough to render the worker irredeemably useless, because everything extra that he knew meant a potential expense and a real loss for the factory. Delia probably said these things in different words, but putting it like this seems closer to her actual thoughts. It wasn't the typical sort of ignorance, the lack of knowledge, experience, or whatever, but rather a positive ignorance, a combination of naivety and contrition. Anyone who wants to become a factory worker knows that he will have to forget many of his skills and acquire others, which belong to a limited sphere and relate to a series of repetitive and relatively simple tasks. I should also say that this renunciation of the self, this "abandonment," was one of the things that made the worker, in my opinion, that which holds up the world.

And so, within the parable that G's life had become, just like F's before it, the time had come to move from one place to another, to wander along lonely paths and through neighborhoods that in some cases had fallen into neglect, with the intention, not always entirely clear and categorical, of dropping the deadweight, of losing the old knowledge that had brought on such an unfortunate end, and, with a little luck, of recovering some general aptitude, a null skill set that would make it possible to embark, from the beginning, on a new phase as a machine operator. G was certainly in this trance when Delia saw him standing on that corner made of nothing, an intersection of dirt and gravel, like someone who had forgotten who he was.

A few hours later she passed the same place on her way back. Before reaching the corner where she had seen G, Delia wondered if he'd still be there, and if so whether it might not be a good idea to talk to him, if only to see how much he still remembered of that other world. But when she got there, G was gone. A distant breeze carried with it the delicate scent of a lot that had once been used to cultivate, I don't know, fruits and vegetables, for example. Now, plants grew there in disarray, in shapes and with smells that, though they alluded to a former domestic use, revealed first and foremost the force of the wild. It was strange to see the way people needed to go back to nothing to reach something that would serve as their refuge from a lack of purpose. Out of an original nothing, like birth, for example, they passed through situations that supplied them with knowledge, habits, and experiences, yet the most likely outcome was that a moment would come when they would have to shake off all they had acquired and start again from zero, that is, to go back to a different nothing and start over. On the way, G could be seen standing on the corner, waiting for something more or less fundamental; he was the epitome of childlike unawareness and, in a certain sense, proletarian naivety. Accustomed to the mechanical commotion of the factory, its world of transmissions, pulleys, and gears, he couldn't figure out what it would take to adapt to his new life of unemployment. But, then, when he really thought about it, he realized that he hadn't really understood the former one, the world of the factory, either, because if he had he would never have been banished. Delia returned with her borrowed clothes, or maybe after restoring them to the collective reserve that provided the community with its best attire; she had completed her errand, but there was no sign of G on the corner . . .

A metal placard, dulled and ravaged by the passage of time, barely visible among the vegetation, belatedly announced that there was "Land for Sale." Actually, the announcement was more primitive than belated; the land had clearly not been for sale for a long time. These places were full of signs just like it; there was no need for Delia to tell me so. At one point, we found ourselves on that corner. She showed me the placard, which was obviously still there, and the exact spot where G had stood, waiting for a sign. To see it, one had to press into the brush, almost colliding with the ancient piece of metal, which had evidently been used for target practice. It was easier to see from a distance when there was a breeze, since the movement of the bushes, and especially their crests, would intermittently reveal it. For some reason I still do not understand, its lettering seemed to Delia to be a proof, presumably of G's opportune presence that afternoon. Seeing G, discovering the sign, not seeing G, forgetting the sign; this had been the succession of Delia's thoughts that afternoon, on this topic, at least. The placard had become the only object that confirmed her version of the story. The land to which the notice referred could have been as vast as the planet itself. Its limits were not visible, at least, not at the time. And so the two of us, but not only us, were at the mercy of contradictory signs in which the recent and distant past intermingled with the long-term and the immediate future, the ephemeral present, and an intolerable perpetuity. I should say that I've never again felt the presence of time so deeply. Sometimes it seemed as definitive as the heavens: implacable, permanent, and constant. Other times it could slip, or string itself out like a lie, a hurried vertigo of contradictory associations. Time was a black hole; it tore us apart and then consumed us, only to leave us—though there was no way to prove this—in the same place from which we were taken.

I could imagine Delia's sadness when she returned to find that G wasn't on the corner anymore. While other people saw the two of them like siblings forced toward the factory by destiny, as I indicated before, Delia saw it differently, though of course with the same intensity. She sensed that something united them, though she didn't know whether it was their age, or another condition. In any event, she was certain that the factory, in banishing him, was responsible for breaking this harmony. And so a set of contradictory feelings was stirred that, resurfacing more intensely at times, stayed with her for a long while. Delia and her peers could feel somewhat responsible for G's absence, but they knew that the ultimate cause was not their factory in particular. The problem lay with the world of the factory as a whole, which did whatever it took to make the workers feel a collective debt for the slightest deviation from the norm, even though in reality it was a world that did as it pleased, followed its own laws, and used machines and workers alike as props in the staging of its own truth. I don't want to abuse the simile, but just as the night was a black hole to those who walked through it, the factory was a black hole to the worker. After isolating, evaluating, and determining what profit could be drawn from them, it hired them, consumed them, and returned them to a life of repetitive actions. One word gives a particularly good sense of it: "exploitation," hiring someone in order to subject them body and soul to a job and, in so doing, squeeze every last drop from them. Delia remembered a gesture: G would unconsciously run his hand through his hair, which meant that something was bothering him. It could be an unusual noise coming from the machine, a lack of coordination among the other workers, or a sudden loss of power: in any event, before looking up or directing his body toward a response, he would lift his right hand—the same one he used to search for crumbs in his breast pocket—and run it through his hair as though he were trying to fix it. And precisely because he was so absorbed, he was making the same gesture when he caught Delia's attention as she passed him on the corner. It's strange that the people closest to Delia, the ones I know, at least, like her friend, should all make that same distinct gesture. Her friend, for example. It was a fluid, rolling movement meant to make the serious less so, to smooth out complexity, and to push affliction, or at least worry, quickly out of mind. It was also a movement meant to conceal surprise. And yet, it was a gesture to which Delia only occasionally resorted.

I've come back from the bathroom, from the mirror in which I observe my belly, indifferent and marked by the years, not unlike the trunk of an old tree. I believe that other people's gestures cling to us like stains, figures left at random on a surface and preserved in our memory through coincidence, unlike the many that are not. I returned to my room with a glass of water; my battered wardrobe faced me from the estuary that opened up at the foot of my bed. I thought about Delia, about the people who were near her, or at least as near to her as I was, and without realizing it, I ran my hand through my hair. What was I after, with this movement? Was I was hoping to uncover something hidden? It's strange; I find that action to be extraordinarily sweet, now. Before, I saw only impatience, vacillation, the urgent sort of nervousness that can be resolved with a gesture, and a theatrical one, at that. Now, though, I see this automatic and therefore invisible movement as an effect of feelings as trite, but from another point of view, as true, or at least lasting, as shyness, pride, humility, and innocence. I see an automatic movement by which the species defends itself, brandishing, shall we say, its dignity. Delia's friend lifted her hand that same way when I found her drawings, and then time and again when she thought, as we waited for Delia, that some indiscretion of mine might slip in through the silence; this was why it was necessary to speak: to keep me from scrutinizing her home. But, as I said earlier, she couldn't find the words. G, too, lifted his hand as he stood alone on that corner: to forgive the afternoon hours that insisted on not passing, to momentarily forget the nothingness that invaded him from below, from the roots under the weeds and the expressionless landscape to every side of him. It didn't occur to me at the time, but now I see that it would have been a miracle if things had been otherwise, if the two of them had not lifted their hands that way in response to something that overwhelmed them, I mean, to something that set them outside themselves, not in the sense of being unaware of their actions, but rather the opposite: of holding those actions up against the awareness that they were acting while only gradually realizing what was happening around them. It should be said that Delia, too, lifted her hand that way, though only a few times, and for a different reason, one somehow less direct and, like everything about her, more complex, sinuous, delicate, and certainly wise.

Delia's friend lifted her hand to her hair on another occasion. It was during that legendary journey, when the man on the train showed her the photo. She made that unusual gesture, which for her only reflected her vacillation, but which the man took as the proof he was waiting for: the figure in the portrait was making a similar one. Seen in that way it seemed like an experiment or a theatrical gesture, which, in a sense, is the nature of photos, thought the man. The problem was that it revealed the full extent of its truth when confronted with reality, that is, when it was set alongside Delia's friend as she enacted the same movement. The performance could have remained a simple performance, but instead it recovered its status as a real act in two senses: that of the person who lifted her hand, even if it was only so that the picture could be taken that way, and that of the person who chose that gesture and no other because it had a specific meaning that she wanted to transmit. And it was this last part, the dual motivation behind both the image and the reality (Delia's friend), that confirmed for the man that they were the same person. G also made the gesture on two definitive occasions. The other one was that ill-fated morning, right after he got to the factory. At first, the young worker didn't understand what was going on, he thought he was in the wrong place, at the wrong workstation, even at the wrong factory. Thinking like a child gradually leaving his infancy behind him, he thought it might have been an innocent prank, a game, but this idea only lasted a moment. If it was a game, it was a short-lived one that ended the moment he realized that its effects would probably last a long time. That was when he ran his hand through his hair. It would be an exaggeration to say that work in the factory came to a halt for a moment, but it would also be a graphic description of what happened. As soon as G lifted his hand to his head, his fellow workers understood that he would leave his post sooner rather than later. Simple and fleeting, though it was also habitual, in this context it was the gesture of someone who could not adapt. The operators who had taken away the old machine and installed the two new ones the night before had made the same gesture more than once during the process, just as thousands of workers do every day. But, as is always the case, a specific set of circumstances distinguished this instance from all others. Perhaps G had only wished to pause at the surprise, the way some people sigh before exerting energy; even so, it was an act that revealed more than it concealed. He made the gesture and began to withdraw. Just as he did on that corner, when it meant that he had withdrawn from everything.

I'm back in my room with a glass of water. I walked down the long hallway of cold tiles, hearing voices through the walls—alert, perhaps because of my footsteps—though the doors remained closed. I went into my room and paused at the estuary, in front of the inlaid panels of my wardrobe doors. A spurious thought came to mind, the slightest of redundancies: I thought something like, "I'm drinking water at the estuary." On the corner of Los Huérfanos, a few feet from where the loading and unloading would take place, there were men who seemed to have trouble walking because of the weight of the merchandise they carried. Sometimes this idea was called into question, when, after one operation and before the next, some would return with their hands empty and an obvious limp. Meanwhile, the animals remained impassive, occasionally letting out a vaporous sigh that became their own measure of time. As I described earlier, it was on this corner that I would wait for Delia every day, wait for her to get off the bus with her uncertain, but firm step. I'd get more anxious with every passing minute; in one of those vagaries of emotions, which themselves can be so muddled, I was afraid she'd never arrive. It was a groundless fear, since no force could divert her; this was proven on several occasions, like when she had to make her way back on foot. I've wondered, sometimes, about my real feelings during those waits. Fear, anxiety, impatience, and so on. Until one afternoon I realized that there was nothing singular about those moments, that the force that made me look forward to the appearance of the bus in the distance, on the corner of Los Huérfanos, was the same one that carried me, in my thoughts, to Delia at every moment. I had fallen into the trance of a continuous date with Delia that she couldn't cancel but which, at any time, some quirk of fate might keep her from attending. At daybreak, just as soon as I had said goodbye to her a few feet from her house, I was already waiting for her, looking forward to seeing her, wondering what I could do to make the time pass quickly and smoothly, that is, without stopping entirely before our next encounter. To say that I waited for her at the corner of Los Huérfanos isn't entirely accurate because, in reality, I was always waiting for her, every minute of every day. Delia was the axis of my thoughts and of my actions, and I existed only insofar as my life related to her. And so, as I observed the efforts of man and beast with their loads, I was overcome by the happy anxiousness of knowing that in just a few moments, my endless waiting, which on days when the hours refused to pass could be bitter and anguished, would be temporarily rewarded.

There were evenings when walking was a pretext not even worth mentioning, because Delia and I were simply waiting for the dense night to fall so we could head to the Barrens. But even though they were a pretext, these aimless strolls had their own weight; they meant more than just the time they passed. I said earlier that to walk with Delia was to witness a change in geography; that nothing was actually altered, and that this made the change all the more evocative and extravagant. It was the same thing that happened with borrowed objects, which increased in value each time they changed hands. As I also wrote before, when Delia wore one particular skirt, whoever saw her would get the impression that it had been made especially for her. The loan flattered her and brought out her best. In a sense, I think, the cut of the skirt was secondary; Delia needed the clothes she wore not to belong to her because that way her own beauty stood out even more. Well, the geography around us was also like this. I would walk along at her side and look at her thick eyebrows, a dense forest in miniature, and then at the other landscape of real trees, the houses, gullies or, in general, the unfinished projects of nature and man; elevated by and more evocative because of Delia's presence, the landscape seemed flawless to me. In short, she was "lending" geography a quality that was then returned to her as though by a mirror, and much to her advantage. It happened with clothing, and it was what happened with the landscape, at the factory, or in any other situation. When Delia wasn't there, the factory seemed empty. The rest of the workers might be at their posts, doing their jobs at the machines, but it would seem like an unplanned strike or a catastrophe had emptied them of meaning and left them spinning their wheels over a void; or the opposite, that the factory had been completely deserted, even though everyone, except Delia, of course, was inside. I've read novels in which places disappear once the character, or protagonist, abandons them. This, which might be called one of the laws of art, can sometimes leave one profoundly uneasy, among other things because geography is never simply a backdrop;

the movement of people through it, even when this falls in the realm of fiction, is what marks the variability and the persistence of the world.

Sometimes a person overcomes this; places, whether they are natural or artificial landscapes, have a harder time outlasting their inhabitants. When a character is lost, abandoned, or simply dead, little remains of him as a sign or promise of his passage through the scene. And when something does remain, it ends up disappearing sooner rather than later. I'll give an example. It involves a man and a woman. She's at an age when most people go to school, but she works in a factory. He's much older, old enough to be her father, though, for a variety of reasons, he never could be. The man has all the typical traits of someone in a novel: undefined age and all that; his character is just a vague impression, as are, shall we say, his voice—in the broadest sense of the word—and his origins. Insignificant beings limited by a complex series of circumstances, they fall in love. But the word "love" is not strong enough. They idolize and worship one another, when they are apart they feel incomplete, that things are less beautiful, happiness unattainable, and so on. During their extended courtship, they discover the vitality of a landscape that had been hidden before, at least to them. It's not so much that they like it, but rather that it seems like the only thing they are in a position to appreciate, or enjoy. The geography is like them: conventional yet difficult to define, somewhere between a half-constructed city and half-cultivated fields, left half completed, abandoned, despondent. The people there seemed to be living in a void. Everything looked as though it had been made with scant resources, grudgingly and from materials that seemed inappropriate at first glance, better suited to be given up than to remain. Both walk through these spaces as solitary beings and, though they're not aware of it, the world watches them. They could go on living this life of nothing forever, but the thing that will inevitably drive them apart is already on its way: she is expecting a child. It's likely that, even without the existence of this child, his abandoning her was already inscribed in the moment they met. Whatever the case, their story takes a significant turn: the man decides to distance himself from the factory worker and, with this, the landscape that served as their backdrop is spent, becoming a useless ornament once the curtain has closed; not unrecognizable, but prosaic. This is what I've been getting at. Is there a way to step outside all this and say, for example, "No, I don't care about the end of the story, their separation, and so on. What I want is for geography to continue on its course until it fully reveals itself, expressing its value in its own terms"?

Walking along those streets that weren't streets and seeing those structures that were either about to become, or to cease being houses, Delia and I were intrigued by the nature of our surroundings. The places we visited, our daily strolls, the passing seasons and the labors of man, and change in general; all this helped prove the reign of the permanent over the variable. Still, we couldn't help but sense the theatricality of those cycles, especially given the regularity with which we frequented those spaces. Here or there, day or night, every place we left felt like a theater set receding behind us, eager to dissolve, sleep, or pause until Delia and I decided to give it life again by returning. This was our impression, which was real, though it ultimately proved false or mistaken. The visits I make now from time to time in the hope of recovering something are a belated indication that this was not the case, that nature did not dissolve or fold in on itself when we abandoned it. The truth is that everything seems more or less the same, recognizable and precise in its simple, natural way. As I said at the beginning, it is unsettling that geography does not change, despite the passage of time; there is something essential about it that remains forever. Many travel diaries and novels, even those that are hundreds of years old, retain an evocative fidelity: there is that tree, that column still stands, the bridge that greets the traveler, the inn that bids him farewell, the marks of the landslide that buries him. The swelling of the river repeats itself, as do the signs of the labors of man. Delia and I saw all this, too; neither of us would have denied the independent existence of reality, and yet we didn't feel the need to believe in it, because every new day and the repetition of every night felt like the first to us. At the same time, by a predictable process of deduction that followed a simple order and an unconscious logic, if every time was the first, there must have been one right before it that had just faded into nothingness. This is why I said before that I never waited for Delia; she was always there, like a heartbeat, being sensed and fading away until the appointed time came and she appeared, small, lovely, and all-encompassing as she was, at my side. Sometimes, as she slept for those few minutes in the shack in the Barrens, I would bury my face in her armpit, also hirsute, into her intoxicating scent. They were categorical smells, strong and differentiated. There was the scent of her body, of course, the most astounding I've known: to say that hers was an animal scent would hardly express it; it blended the smell of a beast in the wild with the sweat of a hard day's work. Her scent could be broken down in several ways, and by breathing each of these in, I felt I had accessed a truth that otherwise would have remained hidden. I found traces: the fabric of her uniform, a substance she worked with in the factory; I even recognized the aroma of a meal, which mixed with and was altered by the taste of her skin. I could hide in the forest of Delia's armpit, I thought. To say nothing of that other, denser, foliage between her legs. Insofar as it centered on abundance, my admiration might seem primitive or elementary, but quantity was only a pretext for my amazement; the truth is that I was transfixed by it as by proof of the divine. I was astonished by the copiousness of Delia's hair, which managed to expand beyond the territory assigned to it, and also by the dark density of the hair itself, which covered her skin so completely that my first response was to wonder what was hidden underneath. And then there was its coarseness, the way it stood on end with the lightest touch like, I don't know, like fine-gauge wire. So it is, I thought as Delia slept, distant from herself: we are replaced by our parts, the fragments better represent the whole of each of us . . .

The material proof of this can be found in the pieces that passed through Delia's hands day after day. Each object retained something of her, a quality that would always be a part of it. I'm not talking about anything allegorical or conceptual, but rather something that was absolutely concrete, though it left no perceptible mark. It was the fact of having been created, at least in part, by Delia's labor. On the average morning she went to work at the factory, she undressed in the narrow hall that served as a changing room, taking off the clothes she had on under her uniform, and walked to her station to carry out the task assigned her. On that morning, as on any other, Delia was resolved to leave a part of herself behind in the fragments and very purpose of her work. Without Delia's sacrifice—represented by her time, her effort, her energy, her meager wages and her part in the collective labor of the factory—without that sacrifice, there was no way production could go on. It was the mark left by all workers. In this case it was Delia who lived on in the commodity, however intangibly. Like a negative halo, made of shadow. In that darkness was hidden everything Delia and the other workers had not received and had not done in order to be able to give life to the object—along with everything, of course, that they *had* done and received, not only so that it could take on all the properties and qualities of a product, but also so that it could become a piece, fundamental to some, of the economic puzzle of everyday life. All those who aren't workers recognize this; they perceive, like an anonymous sign or a warning, the mark of the proletariat on the things they own and use. It is an inescapable addition. And yet it's not an addition, but rather an essential part. Delia knew this, of course. Even if she was unable to argue the point, she understood it through practical knowledge, through experience. This is why objects had a particular nature for her. To give an example, there is the extreme case of the skirt and the fluid nature of property, or the more mundane one of giving up her bus fare home in order to pay, indirectly and symbolically, the weekly installment on a bar of soap. Being unique, objects proliferated through invisible marks; each one was multiplied by the number of instants in a day, a lifetime, and was translated into signs that were often contradictory. The essential nature of commodities was to have a long and complex history, which was, paradoxically, interrupted at their moment of realization; that is, when they became commodities as such. Later, this history lived on in people through these reappearances and symbolic loans. Perhaps this was the source of the collective attachment to objects—the fact that they retained the marks of other ways of being used and handled, both unknown and essential, without which they would lose their true value.

Now that I'm standing at the estuary in my room I remember, through a straightforward association, Delia's own inverted estuary.

It opened like a fan from her anus, ascending her groin and spreading beyond its borders. A dizzying territory. It advanced upward, laying claim to the surface of her skin until it reached its unexpected and, I suppose, astonishing end when, overcome by a sudden weakness, it became a simple and sparse trail of down that slid into her bellybutton, almost entirely spent. Now the wardrobe, the bed, and the chair are there, as is the window that lets in a light as solid and as dense as a block. At nightfall or, rather, sometime after that, in the middle of the night, after taking even more steps across this river of wood, a light will come on in the window where, a few days ago, someone struggled to survive. It has often seemed to me that much of a person's life is filled with thoughts that have no future. Observing a flickering flame, counting the days left in the week, readying oneself for the shock of cold metal. And this is only the beginning, by which I mean that one could also start from the premise that all thoughts are without a future because they are made to hold up a dead moment; some more obviously than others, though they all end up muddled together in their futility. I can sit on the edge of my bed and wait for night to come while staring at the walls, trying to make out what the voices that can be heard on the other side are saying. On days like this, I'm surprised by the direction my thoughts take, how they shift from one thing to another and, without warning, lead me to wonder about Delia's fate. The word "fate" has rarely seemed more appropriate to me. I could have written Delia's "future," but that future would now be, in the strictest sense, the past. Fate, on the other hand, whether it has been fulfilled or not, always asserts itself as an unknown. I should say that when I left her, Delia's reaction was so wise that, though it provoked no feeling in me then, it gradually filled me with shame. More and more, in fact; even years later, when it could be said that time should have helped the work of forgetting along, her memory moved me, and then filled me with a burning shame. Still, I had no regrets, nor did I pity Delia. Tenderness, as is well known, does not last long. It's hard for something like tenderness to endure under any circumstances, even when the tenderest of moments is repeated. But not shame. A well-deserved feeling of shame can stay with us our whole lives, and it's not uncommon to find shame that has been passed intact from generation to generation. As the verse goes, "The girl held, in the gleam of her dark hair, the trembling gaze that shamed the lad." Delia took to waiting for me in the most improbable places, though not exactly in order to surprise me. I said a while ago that she was a simple creature, but I also said she was wise. With her silence and her patience she was trying to tell me that she didn't need to speak, that the place she chose to wait and the openness of her gaze were signs enough. No matter how often this scene was repeated, how many encounters there were just like it, silent and cut short by my flight, the frankness of her gaze was unfailing. She watched for a reaction from me like someone searching for a sign of life. I evaded her, at first with my eyes and then with my body, by changing course. She never spoke; she only followed me with her gaze. She had the deranged air of a victim about her. To a stranger, she probably looked like a lost soul.

Her growing belly did not stop her. To me she seemed sweeter, rounder, and— as often happens with pregnant women—lovelier, holding up her pregnancy on legs as straight as sticks, always waiting, always with the same wistful expression. There was bewilderment in her gaze, that much was easy to see, but it was also free of demands. It was simply a gaze that wanted to be told that it was all just a bad dream, a storm that was slow to pass. Her wisdom consisted of this, and it was this that ended up making me feel ashamed.

Because she made no demands of me, it was as though she were turning the other cheek while her swelling stomach offered growing proof of her dignity. She would show up alongside the thistle barrens, across from the bus stop on the corner of Los Huérfanos, just a few feet from the gully where we had seen F's boys, on the corner (if it could be called that) of her friend's house, and so on. As though Delia, in her need to get my attention back, understood that she needed to bring geography up to date: these were no longer the places we visited together, but rather where she had ended up waiting for me, day after day. I should also say that her strength and determination flustered me, and I responded viscerally, abruptly; I wanted the earth to swallow me whole and I fled without knowing where I was headed, only that I needed to get out of there, to get far away.

This might sound a little inappropriate, but I don't think I'm far from the truth when I say that if Delia acted this way, it was because of her proletarian nature. As I said, few human tasks have turned resignation or waiting into an essential trait, a virtue, even. Yet this is the first thing one notices in the worker, and it is what endures in them. People often talk about the patience of farmers, the endless periods of waiting that the land endures, of the seasons weaving themselves together into a single era in which we are no more than a grain of sand in the universe, and so on, but they rarely mention the infinite patience of the worker and the intractable presence of the machines. This is because of their operational cycles, which are always visible and always repeated, and because of the transmission of energy, which, by translating itself into force, imposes the idea of a process that is unstoppable, endless, and above all, unfathomable. The legends that depict the fragility of machines, like the one in which they are destroyed by nothing more than the carelessness of those operating them, actually draw attention to the opposite, to the continuity of the machinery, which is its greatest strength, in the face of which all else recedes. The land is always telling us that it could disappear at any time, that the ground is no more solid than our perception of it. Industry, on the other hand, promises to operate forever, imposing itself on everything associated with it. Anyway, whether it is a force the worker assigns to the machines or a force that flows in the opposite direction, from the machine to the mind of the worker, what is certain is that, while the strength Delia showed by waiting any and everywhere, regardless of the weather, could be attributed to the surprise she carried in her heart—to put it one way—but it was also nourished by that intractable strength that came from her proletarian condition. Because she had a talent for showing up right in front of me, and because I obviously had to see her before I could avert my eyes, I was able to see how evenly her belly was growing. She was so young that the pregnancy paradoxically emphasized her innocence, making her seem like a girl who had discovered the secret of the game, or like prey that was not granted the hunter's mercy. And so Delia's belly grew and grew. Toward the end, I'd see her waiting for me, leaning up against whatever was at hand—a post, a tree, a fence, or a wall—until one day, feeling my shame ebb away, I noticed that she wasn't there. She and the child had stepped into the dark.

Sergio Chejfec, originally from Argentina, has published numerous works of fiction, poetry, and essays. Among his grants and prizes, he has received fellowships from the Civitella Ranieri Foundation in 2007 and the John Simon Guggenheim Foundation in 2000. He currently teaches in the Creative Writing in Spanish Program at NYU. His novels, *The Planets* (a finalist for the 2013 Best Translated Book Award in fiction) and *My Two Worlds*, are both available from Open Letter in English translation.

Heather Cleary is a translator of fiction, criticism, and poetry, whose work has appeared in journals including *Two Lines*, *Habitus*, *The Coffin Factory*, and *New York Tyrant*, and in the edited volumes *Revealing Mexico* and *The Film Edge*. In 2005, she was awarded a Translation Fund grant from the PEN America Center for her work on Oliverio Girondo's *Persuasioón de los días*. She is also the founding editor of the *Buenos Aires Review*. In addition to *The Dark*, she translated Chejfec's *The Planets*.

O pen Letter—the University of Rochester's nonprofit, literary translation press—is one of only a handful of publishing houses dedicated to
increasing access to world literature for English readers. Publishing ten titles in
translation each year, Open Letter searches for works that are extraordinary and
influential, works that we hope will become the classics of tomorrow.

Making world literature available in English is crucial to opening our cultural
borders, and its availability plays a vital role in maintaining a healthy and
vibrant book culture. Open Letter strives to cultivate an audience for these
works by helping readers discover imaginative, stunning works of fiction and
poetry, and by creating a constellation of international writing that is engaging,
stimulating, and enduring.

Current and forthcoming titles from Open Letter include works from Bulgaria,
Denmark, France, Germany, Italy, Latvia, Poland, Russia, and many other
countries.

www.openletterbooks.org